PARIS, CALIFORNIA

Novels by Kevin St. Jarre

Aliens, Drywall, and a Unicycle

Celestine

The Twin

Absence of Grace

The Book of Emmaus

PARIS, CALIFORNIA

KEVIN ST. JARRE

Encircle Publications
Farmington, Maine, U.S.A.

Hardback ISBN 13: 978-1-64599-407-7
Paperback ISBN 13: 978-1-64599-409-1
E-book ISBN 13: 978-1-64599-408-4

Library of Congress Control Number (LCCN): 2022943284

Cover design and digital illustration by Deirdre Wait
Cover photographs © Getty Images

Published by:

Encircle Publications
PO Box 187
Farmington, ME 04938

info@encirclepub.com
http://encirclepub.com

For Guy St. Jarre,
intelligent and kind, who can fix anything,
who sets, by example, an impossibly high standard of
work-ethic, who laughs and makes others laugh,
and who raised us right.
Love you, Dad

1

Ashin Asilomar lived in Paris, in the midcoastal region of California, where the weather was perfect, but the ocean water was too cold for most. Tucked in, north of Big Sur, south of Santa Cruz, not quite on the Monterey Peninsula, but not really off of it either.

It had the red tile roofs and stucco one comes to expect from the region, but it was not famous for wine, nor garlic, nor butterflies. Paris's streets were still walkable, and the local schools were decent. It was not really a tourist destination, but not immune to them either.

Ashin had been born here, grew up in its schools, went away only to get a college education, and came back with a wife. He had set himself up there, changing locations only once when he gave in to new road construction that was supposed to modernize the town. It had not only displaced his dental practice, but destroyed the wide sidewalks and greenspace on that side of town. The project had eliminated a bakery, a butchery, and a barbershop.

With those gone, many of the neighborhood's residents had left, too. That part of town was now little more than a strip mall next to a road where traffic moved too quickly for pedestrians to cross.

But Ashin had thrived after relocating, and he jokingly gave much of the credit to candy shops down by the antique carousel. He and his wife, Rebecca, had been able to buy a small home, with its own red tile roof and stucco walls, only a couple streets up from the Pacific Ocean. On warmer nights, he fell asleep listening to sea lions barking down by the wharf.

He eventually retired and, despite all the plans, he lost Rebecca shortly thereafter. They had never had children, and he had no other family within 1,000 miles.

The day she passed, he had lifted her hand into his own. It was so frail; the skin a delicate paper. Her fingers were long, slender, and still soft despite their weathered appearance. He knew every millimeter of her hand, having held it so many times. At their wedding, as they had first walked through this house together, and they had held hands while watching wonders like man walking on the moon, at graduations, at other weddings, funerals, and then through that horrific moment when she was told she had cancer. He had held her hand through months of grueling treatment.

That horrible day, his eyes had traced the line of her arm up to her tiny shoulder, further still to her face. He had watched as she lay sleeping, with labored breath, but at least the hospital equipment was finally gone. No more needles in her willowy arms. The alarms of occluded IVs were at last absent. Her once thick hair, by that time, had been replaced with only wisps of grey, and her scalp clearly visible. Her face, once so replete with life and color, was gaunt and pale. Yet, to him, she had been every bit as exquisite as the day he first saw her, all those decades before.

A stout candle had breathed the scent of jasmine throughout the room from one corner. He sat on a diminutive wooden rocker, too small for him, as he watched over her while she slept. Her head, ever so gradually, began to move. She turned her face and her lips parted. Her eyes, with tremendous effort, opened. They were the color of the sweetest chocolate, they reminded him of soft velvet. Her lips barely moved, but he heard her whisper, and heard her request.

"Music," she had said. Exhausted at the effort her eyes closed again, her head settling back, mouth relaxing.

He reached out to the nightstand, beyond a clock-radio with its luminescent green numbers, to a jewelry box. It was old and rectangular, with corners cut. The lid was oversized, larger than the opening. The wood was maple, with an inlay of flowers on the lid. He lifted it and turned the silver key on its bottom. He placed the jewelry box back on the nightstand, and carefully opened the lid. A tinny music began to emanate from it.

"Greensleeves" began to play. It was the only sound in the room save her breathing. He took her hand once more, and began to sing to her. His voice was raspy from days of hard tears. He stopped singing, with his sorrow choking off his breath. He lowered his damp brow to her hand as he held it, and lying there, he wept quietly, and knew she was gone.

That jewelry box sat in the living room now. He very rarely opened it, but there it was, and he would look at it from time to time. He no longer cried at the sight of it, but he missed her.

If one had to be on his own, though, Paris, California, was an okay place to do it. The coldest night of the year got down to about 40°F, and the warmest day of the year might reach for 90°F. It rained mostly at night, was foggy in the mornings, and the afternoons were sunny. The air was never quite dry, and rarely ever humid. Paris was a wonderful place, climatologically.

Ashin could walk down to the shore. If the winds were right, towering white plumes of seawater would spray up off the same rocks that had eaten wooden ships as far back as the 17th century. Looking out, he'd see the tops of the kelp forest, and maybe an otter, floating on its back, using a stone to crack abalone on its chest.

The walks were nice exercise, a way to get fresh air, but they also helped with his diabetes. When Ashin had first been diagnosed, his doctor told him that he might be able to manage his condition without insulin by simply going for a walk each day. He took the advice, and so far, it had helped.

Paris had lovely parks, especially Wilson Point, whose grassy spaces fell to boulders that spilled into the ocean. Cypress trees pushed deep green into the cobalt-blue skies. People walked the perimeter while watching the surf come in. Some threw Frisbees to family members, or to unleashed dogs. Those with different breeds would compare and compliment.

People picnicked on blankets, even the dogless, and when a big-headed Labrador would come in to sniff a sandwich, they were often met with a smile and a crust of bread.

Artists met, and painted *en plein air.* Almost every day, a busker or two would play guitar, or even flute or violin.

The community shared the beaches and places like Wilson Point Park. There was no rancor; there were only people and animals living in the same spaces.

2

As Ashin sat on his front porch one morning, a large silver SUV pulled up in front of his neighbor's overgrown lawn. A diminutive man with gray hair climbed down out of it, scurried around to the back, and pulled out a sign. With this, he walked into the middle of the Kintners' front yard, and drove the sign into the ground. He looked up and spotted Ashin.

"Hey Doc," he called.

"Hey Mitch, how's it going?" Ashin asked.

"It's going," Mitch said, and wiped his forehead with his hand.

"Going to try to sell it, huh?" Ashin asked.

"Do my best," Mitch said.

"Might help to mow," Ashin said.

Leon Kintner would have never let the lawn get that high. It hadn't looked like a green on a golf course, but he had mowed it once a week and kept it tidy. Ashin had watched the Kintner kids grow up in that yard and eventually move on to their own lives. After Mrs.

Kintner had her strokes and passed, Leon went to live with one of his daughters in San Diego. That last night before he left, Leon had come over and the two of them shared a beer on the front porch.

Leon had said, "I gotta go for the air down there, in San Diego."

"I suppose you do," Ashin replied, but both men knew the air in Paris was perfect and pleasant, and so they said nothing more about it. The next day, Leon just stared at the house from the backseat as the car pulled away. Ashin waved, but if Leon saw him, there was no sign.

There was certainly a sign now, 'FOR SALE,' standing in Leon's former lawn.

"I'll send my son over to mow," Mitch said, "Enjoying retirement?"

"Doing just fine," Ashin said. Unlike many retirees, Ashin hadn't launched on a year of travel, or bought a lakeside cabin, or an RV and taken up a nomadic existence. Ashin knew that having a plan for after retirement was important, but not a bucket list of things people frantically do, as if retirement is the picking of a plant that will soon wilt and be gone. He thought if someone wanted to take a long-postponed trip, that was great, but a list with tick boxes dragging a newly retired person around the world in search of the Great Pyramid of Giza, walking the Great Wall of China, climbing Machu Picchu, snowmobiling in Aroostook County, or gazing at the Taj Mahal seemed more like a source of stress than the celebration of a milestone reached.

Ashin had instead planned to make sure to eat well,

to keep doing puzzles, to spend some time on the front porch every day, or as least as often as possible, to see other people, and to continue to read the newspaper. He set himself a bed time, and a wake time, and tried to stick to them without being a perfectionist. He resolved to shower at least two out of three days, and for God's sake to brush his teeth. Every dentist should die with a mouthful of his own teeth, Ashin believed.

Maybe someday, he'd plan a trip somewhere distant, but his plan included his walks down to the park and whatnot.

"Go for your walk today?" Mitch asked, "Big surf. Take care." He turned away and began climbing into his SUV, the way a child might mount his father's overstuffed armchair. Ashin smiled at the effort. He knew Mitch Mitchell to be a good guy, and an honest man. The vehicle was simply a bit oversized.

* * *

Within a couple days, cars were driving by the Kintner place at a crawl, with faces pressed to windows. People in them were pointing, attempting to square dreams with potential. Most of the cars had out-of-state plates, which was odd. For decades, Californians had moved away to Nevada, Oregon, and Colorado, but few out-of-staters had moved to a small town like Paris.

Just as surprising, less than two weeks later, Ashin arrived home from his walk just in time to see Mitch's SUV pulling away. On top of the lawn sign was a new placard that read, "SOLD," and within days, a moving truck appeared. The hum-ants carried furniture and boxes into the house.

Ashin assumed that the man carrying half as much, but talking twice as much, was the new owner. He was explaining couch history to the movers, who nodded as if they cared, and then he told the story of the dining room table. A woman poked her head out the door of the house, but said nothing before disappearing back inside. Ashin wasn't sure if she had been looking, or sniffing, but he knew his own wife would've been the one in the yard.

Ashin didn't think Rebecca would've carried a thing, but she would've been a much more gracious host. He imagined she would've set up a TV stand on the front lawn, just out of the way, with a pitcher of lemonade and glasses. Also, as men carried a sofa, she wouldn't have been concerned with its destination, or even really its care, but she would have been cautioning the men about the bottom step, or to lift with their knees and not their backs.

When Ashin and Rebecca had moved into this home together, she had purchased a case of root beer, frowning on Ashin's idea of providing actual beer, and shared it with the four men who unloaded the truck. Rebecca had made such a fuss, that the men felt obliged to drink all sixteen bottles, and the result was that with every heavy lift there was an accidental belch, and there were a great many trips to the bathroom.

When, near the end of the job, the youngest man said to his coworkers that he was hungry, Rebecca immediately invited the four to stay for supper. Mr.

Varney, of Varney Movers, was among the four and quickly snapped at the young man to mind his manners and get to work, but then with the sweetest smile, turned to Rebecca, and politely declined the supper invitation.

When Rebecca began to insist they stay, making Varney noticeably uncomfortable, only then did Ashin say anything. He thought that the more Rebecca insisted, the worse it would be for the kid who had initially accepted the dinner offer. Ashin only said, "Honey," with a slight nod, and she read him perfectly.

"Perhaps another time," Rebecca had said with a smile.

Varney smiled broadly with relief, and said, "Thank you," and went out to see what was left to bring in.

With the new neighbors, all these years later, Ashin could see no such magnanimity. Walking from the backyard came a boy—not a small child, but not a man either. He walked to the truck, but didn't offer to help. A mover came over with a bicycle, a large metal basket over its rear fender. The bike was a bit too short for the boy, but the mover set it down, and then patted his shoulder. When the mover returned to the truck, Ashin could see the boy's shoulders drop, and then he wheeled it toward the garage, disappearing around the corner of the house.

Mitch pulled up in front of Ashin's, not wanting to get in the way of the work. He came around the SUV, approached Ashin, and as he began to climb the steps, he asked, "Have you met your new neighbors, yet?"

"I'm not selling my house, Mitch," Ashin said.

"I know it, I know it," Mitch said.

"I haven't met them, but I've seen them," Ashin said.

"But if you were thinking about selling the house, we had a lot of offers on that one before the Funks turned in the best bid," Mitch said, "the house sold quick, and it wasn't exactly a dream home. They're planning some pretty significant renovations."

"The Funks?" Ashin asked.

"That's the family name—Funk. They're okay. Maybe a bit high-strung," Mitch said, "Especially for Paris."

Ashin looked that way and watched the boxes streaming in. *High-strung for Paris*, thought Ashin. *Great.*

3

He pulled his sweater off the peg, but then put it back. Instead, he chose a floppy hat that seemed to be made of the same canvas as his sneakers, which he just as often referred to as tennis shoes, although they'd never seen a tennis court.

As he left his steps, and headed down the sidewalk, he heard someone behind him.

"Where are you going?"

Ashin turned, and saw the new neighbor boy standing there, hands relaxed at his sides, weight equally distributed on both feet.

"Good morning," Ashin said.

"Good morning. Can I come with you?" the boy asked.

Ashin thought for a moment, and then said, "You don't know where I'm going."

"That's why I asked that first, but you didn't answer, so I thought it would be rude to ask again," the boy said.

Ashin's eyebrows rose, and he asked, "What's your name?"

"Mateo Funk," he said, and then added, "Sir."

"Well, Mateo, nice to meet you, I'm Dr. Asilomar," he said.

"You're a doctor?"

"A retired dentist."

"Oh," Mateo said, sounding a bit disappointed.

"You don't like dentists?" Ashin asked.

"I've never been to one. What's it like to have your hands in other people's mouths?" Mateo asked.

Ashin said, "Wet."

Mateo said nothing, and blinked.

"What about not talking to strangers?" Ashin asked.

"We're neighbors," Mateo said.

Ashin looked to the Funk house, and then back at the boy. "In that case, you don't have to call me 'Sir.' Come on, let's go for a walk," Ashin said.

Mateo asked, "Where to?"

"Here," Ashin said.

"Huh?" Mateo asked.

"At the end of the walk, we'll be here," Ashin said, and smiled.

Mateo nodded, as if he got it, and they began walking down the road. Neither spoke for quite some time, which suited Ashin just fine. It was nice to meet a young person who was okay with the quiet. Actually, it was Ashin who spoke first.

"So, where did you move from?" Ashin asked.

"West Texas," Mateo said.

"Ah, that explains it."

Mateo asked, "Explains what?"

"Most people have been moving out of California.

But, if you're starting from Texas, it makes sense," Ashin said.

"You don't like Texas?" Mateo asked.

"Did you like it?" Ashin asked.

"It was normal," the boy said. "Flat as far as the eye could see. If you were away from houses, you could see forever. Just a gnarled mesquite tree here and there in the way. In this place, the whole town slopes into the ocean. I mean, how do kids learn to ride their bikes on the side of a hill like this?"

"Your bike is too small for you," Ashin said.

"You saw it? I outgrew it. Probably safer that way," Mateo said. He held his arms outstretched and level, but then pitched with the angle of the avenues as they crossed the streets, on their way to the Pacific.

"You'll get used to it," Ashin said.

"Is that what we're supposed to do?" Mateo asked.

"What?"

"When things change… we get used to it?" Mateo asked.

"I think so," Ashin said, "You said you got used to Texas. What's the alternative?"

Mateo said, "Leave."

They walked along, and then saw a group of children, a bit younger than Mateo, wearing wet suits and carrying short surfboards. They left the sidewalk, and walked along a well-worn path that ran diagonally across a front lawn, disappearing around a large house and, of course, headed downhill.

"They all live there?" Mateo asked.

Ashin looked over at the kids and said, "That's Linda

McDougal's house. None of those kids live there."

"They walked right across her lawn," Mateo said.

Tired of being nudged onto the grass as Mateo looked this way and that while walking, Ashin switched sides with the boy.

"They wore a groove in the grass," Mateo added.

Ashin said, "That path has been there forever. They walked over her lawn because that's where the path to the beach is. That groove was there when theLoracks built the house, it was there when the Shidhausers bought the place, and it was there when the McDougals moved in."

"Awful nice of the McDougals to let them keep doing it," Mateo said.

Ashin was bit confused. "Let them?"

"Hey, those are cool," Mateo said, pointing upward.

Ashin looked up, and said, "Those are seagulls. Long wings, eh?"

Mateo, looking straight up as he walked, bumped into Ashin again, this time pushing him off the sidewalk. Ashin looked at Mateo, and sighed.

"Sorry," Mateo said with a shrug.

Walking again, Ashin asked, "Any brothers and sisters?"

"I have a sister, Elizabeth-Marie," Mateo said.

"Are you a good big brother?" Ashin asked.

"She's much older, is only my half-sister, and she moved out already," Mateo said.

"How old are you?" Ashin asked.

"I'm twelve. I don't even remember spending time with her, really, but I'm told when she left it caused me to have separation anxiety," Mateo said.

"You're a bit different, aren't you?" Ashin asked.

Mateo said, "Don't worry, I don't find that rude. My gram, that's my mom's grandmother, used to always say, 'Protect your inner-weird.' She was different."

"I believe you," Ashin said. "Would you like to see the beach?"

"Sure," Mateo said, and they both headed for the McDougals' lawn.

4

The path wound down to the beach, which was only 300 feet long, and walnut-sized stones were scattered about on the sand. The kids with the boards were already in the waves. Rock walls rose up about eight feet, framed the beach on three sides, and extended into the water. The funnel effect caused the waves to be a bit more dramatic than they otherwise might have been. Above these short cliffs sat three large houses, each with huge windows facing the ocean. Wooden steps came down the face of rock, but only halfway to the beach. They hung there, suspended, with the bottom step chest high above the sand.

A woman approached with a border collie at her heels. Mateo watched as the dog and woman went by. "That dog had no leash," Mateo said, "I'm not scared of dogs. I'm just saying."

Someone cried out behind them, and they both looked back in time to see a surfer upside down in the air, almost as high as his surfboard was, before disappearing into the waves. His friends laughed and clapped as they sat straddling their own boards.

Ashin and Mateo continued on, and when in front of the third house, Mateo pointed at it and asked, "Isn't this their beach?"

"Everything below the wrack line belongs to everybody," Ashin said.

"What's a wrack line?" Mateo asked.

"You know what high tide is?" Ashin asked.

"Of course," Mateo said.

"The highest point that the tide reaches, that line, see that kelp up there? The highest point of high tide is the wrack line," Ashin said.

"So, any part of the beach that ends up underwater at high tide is owned by everyone?" Mateo asked.

"Exactly. Otherwise, at high tide, these homeowners would own part of the ocean. No one should ever own the ocean," Ashin said. "I mean, Maine and Massachusetts have some weird law about 'fishing, fowling, and navigation' or whatever, but in the reasonable states, it's that way."

He saw the boy looking down the wrack line. "What are you thinking?" Ashin asked.

"At high tide, there's not much beach here, is there?" Mateo asked.

"Not much," Ashin said.

They walked on, and as they left the beach on the far end, there was another path that switched back up the cliff, across yet another lawn, and then a dirt road. They began climbing its slope.

"Why isn't this road paved?" Mateo asked.

"It's private," Ashin said.

"It's not a town road?" Mateo asked.

"This was all a saltwater farm once. Someone bought it, passed it down to the next generation, who turned it into a neighborhood, building and selling these houses, and they even constructed the road that runs through," Ashin said.

"There's more space in Texas," Mateo said.

Ashin almost asked what Mateo meant by this, but didn't. Instead, he asked, "Ever heard of a paper road?"

"What is it?" Mateo asked.

"It's when a road only exists on paper. For example, towns that were just forming, brand new, were laying out where the roads would be. That way, when people built their houses, they wouldn't be scattered all over, because they could ask the town where the planned roads would be," Ashin said.

"So, paper roads were planned, are town property, but never built?" Mateo asked.

"Right, because they sort of over-planned," Ashin said.

"Maybe if they built the roads now, more people would move in?" Mateo asked.

"Well, it's much harder now. Many of the fanciest houses, with large yards right along the shore, those paper roads run through those lots. A lot of paper roads were right up against the shoreline. Today, people have lawns, hedges, pools, and gazebos that are right on top of a paper road," Ashin said.

"They built without asking the town," Mateo said.

"To be fair, the property might have been in the

family's hands before the current owner was even born. Why would anyone suspect that their lawn is on a road that only exists on paper, in a government drawer somewhere," Ashin said.

"It doesn't make it right. The town should go out and mark all the paper roads, and make people take their pools off of them," Mateo said.

"What the heck for?" Ashin said.

"It's town property," Mateo said, "It belongs to everyone. Like the beach below high tide."

"Mateo, the beach has always been in use by everyone. If it suddenly were taken away, that would be horrible. But, that twelve-foot wide strip of land that runs through people's yards, used only by those families for generations, that's not depriving the public of anything," Ashin said.

"Still not right," Mateo said.

"Pick your fights. We lose something when we cling to the letter of the law instead of the spirit of the law," Ashin said.

They made their way up to the paved surfaces, and looped back toward home. Mateo started to say something once, but stumbled on a sidewalk segment, and recovered without falling or speaking.

5

Ashin put a little sugar in his coffee. He only did this with the first cup of the morning; the second cup would be black and unsweetened. He thought it was a way to cut his sugar intake. While he was stirring, there was a knock at the screen door. The inside door was wide open, so when he looked over, he could see Mateo staring in through the screen.

"Are you walking today?" Mateo asked.

Holding up his cup, Ashin said, "I'll have a cup or two first."

Mateo didn't respond, he just continued to stare into the house. Ashin headed toward the door, and had to pause for Mateo to understand that he was coming through. Stepping out, Ashin moved over to one of the porch chairs and sat, and then motioned for Mateo to take the other.

"Do you always get up early?" Ashin asked.

Mateo shrugged.

Ashin took a hot sip, and asked, "What do you do

during the day? Have you made any friends?"

"There are no kids here," Mateo said.

"It's tough to arrive when school isn't in session. I'm sure you'll meet plenty this fall," Ashin said.

"But there are no other teenagers in this neighborhood. Even those kids who went surfing don't live on this street," he said.

"Well, Paris is a town that young families sometimes find hard to get into," Ashin said.

"They have rules against young people?" Mateo asked.

"The houses are expensive for people just starting out. By the time folks have gotten to a point in their lives where they can afford homes here, their kids are often grown up," Ashin said. "From what I'm seeing in the newspaper these days, looks like prices are only going up."

"We moved here," Mateo said.

"What does your father do for a living?" Ashin said.

"He's a newspaper reporter. They don't make that much," Mateo said.

"And your mom?"

"She's a quant," Mateo said.

"I'm sorry?"

"You know, she analyzes quantitative data, on her computer, using algorithms she created and genetically optimized to manage these hedge funds," Mateo said.

Ashin's mouth fell open.

"What?" Mateo asked.

"Are you some kind of alien?" Ashin asked.

"Huh?"

Ashin shook his head, and said, "So, that's how your family could afford to buy here."

"And you were a dentist," Mateo said.

"I'm still a dentist. I'm retired. But when I bought here, houses were reasonably priced," Ashin said.

Mateo leaned back in his chair, and one knee started bouncing.

"What is it?" Ashin asked.

"If you go for a walk before I come back, can you come get me?" Mateo asked.

"Where are you going?" Ashin asked.

Mateo said, "I'll go eat breakfast. I didn't eat because I was worried that you'd leave without me, but it seems like I have time."

"Go eat. I'll come get you," Ashin said.

Without a word, Mateo got up, went down the steps, and walked across the yard and into his house. Ashin shook his head again, and took another sip. *What an odd duck*, he thought.

6

He was putting his coffee cup in the sink, having had his second already, when Monique Cyr Hamilton Kirschner arrived. She knocked, didn't wait for an answer, and as she entered, she caught her bucket in the closing screen door.

"Ah crap," she said, freeing it, turning, and only then seeing Ashin. "Oh! Dr. Asilomar, sorry, you startled me."

"Not too messy today, Ms. Kirschner. I tried to keep up with it this week," Ashin said.

"We'll see if I can't put a shine on everything for you," she said. "I have a couple of leftovers for you as well. I'll put those right in your freezer." She was a tiny thing, and looked like she could've sat in the bucket she carried around. It seemed her pants were a different color each visit, but always the same exact style, with pork chop pockets. Ashin knew that by the time she left, he'd be able to smell the Pine-Sol from the sidewalk.

"Thank you. I washed your Tupperware from last

time," he said. If it was a container that held leftover food, Ashin called it "Tupperware." It didn't matter if it were Pyrex glass or a repurposed plastic margarine container.

"Oh, you didn't have to, but thanks," she said.

Ashin walked past her to the door, and started to put his shoes on.

"Going for a walk?" she asked.

"That's right. See you in a little while," he said, reaching for the screen door.

"Alright," she said.

After Rebecca passed, there was a period of time when her friends had cooked more food for Ashin than he could possibly eat, and they even came over a few times to clean. Before they would arrive, Ashin would try to pick up the place, simply because he knew Rebecca wouldn't want them seeing the house a mess. Eventually, as time passed, they brought less food, and no one was cleaning—not even Ashin. Dishes were washed less often, and the only cleaning of the floor was spot mopping when he spilled something. Until one morning when he'd woken up and made some coffee, but then realized that half-a-dozen mugs were dirty. There was only one tablespoon left in the drawer. Spills on the counter had been wiped, but not washed. There were pans within pans on the stove. He saw an empty glass on the coffee table next to an unused coaster, and a box of saltines. It wasn't spilled, or even open. After all, he hadn't become a complete slob, but Rebecca wouldn't have liked it.

So, he called one of her friends, Kathleen, for a recommendation for a housekeeper. Of course, Kathleen offered to do it herself, but eventually relented and recommended Ms. Kirschner.

Ashin suspected that Ms. Kirschner had been fully briefed by Kathleen, and that she had been recommended in no small part because of the natural caretaker she would be, in addition to a thorough housekeeper. He was grateful for her help, even though he paid for it. Still, he dearly missed Rebecca. A house filled with the aroma of Windex, Pledge, and Pine Sol, and even a freezer full of casserole and lasagna in pseudo-Tupperware, was certainly no replacement for her.

He walked down the steps, across the lawn, and onto the Kintner porch. *The Funk porch*, he thought. He knocked, and waited. He knocked again.

The door opened, and the man who had directed the furniture delivery was standing there.

"Yes?" he asked.

"My name is Ashin Asilomar. I'm your neighbor, so first, I'd like to welcome you to the neighborhood," Ashin said, and extended his hand.

The man took it, smiled broadly, and said, "Thank you. My name is Deepak Funk. Nice to meet you."

"You as well. Uh, this might seem a bit odd, but I'm also here because Mateo said he wanted to know when I was leaving for my daily walk. He joined me once, and I guess he didn't find it too boring," Ashin said.

Deepak's smile never faded, and he said, "Sure, sure, he told us you showed him a way to the nearby beach. Terrific. Maybe today you could show him the way to the downtown."

Ashin asked, "What downtown?"

Deepak chuckled, and said, "Yeah, yeah, I know what you mean. These little towns. A coffee shop, a bookstore, a market, and a divorce attorney, eh?"

Ashin's brow furrowed. *They bought a house without checking out the town?* he wondered? "I'm sorry, I'm afraid Paris really doesn't have a downtown per se. We have two gas stations. There are some stubborn candy shops near the carousel, the shuttered canneries, and a closed dental office. Oh, and a public library, open every other day," he said.

Deepak's smile faded a bit. "No coffee shop?"

"On the far edge of town, farthest from the ocean and closer to the interstate, there's a hospital, and a strip mall, but not much in it. And it's certainly not walking distance. People around here have been clamoring for new businesses for years, but we haven't changed much, I'm afraid. More have closed than have opened. You can drive over to Carmel. That little town is nothing but nice little shops," Ashin offered.

"Great. Great. Okay, Mateo, right?" he said, and then forced a laugh. Over his shoulder, he called for his son, and Mateo soon appeared.

"Ready?" Ashin asked.

Mateo nodded and stepped out past his father.

"Nice to meet you," Ashin said.

"You too," Deepak said, and closed the door.

Ashin and Mateo went a different way this time, and although the boy didn't ask, Ashin said, "We're going to the park today. Wilson Point Park. We can even sit a bit, look out at the ocean."

"Okay," Mateo said.

7

The first half of a walk in Paris was almost always downhill, and it made the going pretty easy. The park appeared before them, the ocean wide open behind it, and not walled in as it had been at the beach with the houses.

Ashin noticed that the movement within the park, the rhythm, was different. Instead of the free flow of active people, and dogs moving around those at rest and picnicking, there were people standing in clumps and in a line.

"Is there a show or something?" Mateo asked.

"I'm not sure," Ashin said, "Let's take a look."

They walked through the bystanders, and arrived at a fence that had never been there before. It was waist high to Ashin, and he lay his hand on the top of it. He could see that it ran in a square, and inside that square were two people, and two dogs. The only dogs at Wilson Point Park, where there normally would have been at least half-a-dozen.

Mateo pointed at a sign, hanging from the fence, and read, "Off-leash dog area. Dogs must be on a leash until inside the designated area."

Ashin surveyed the space; it was perhaps thirty feet across. It was then that he saw her, standing at one corner, smiling. Approaching her, Ashin said, "Well, Almira, you did it, but I want you to know how awful I think you are for doing it."

"Ashin! You know it's a safety issue. Disgusting, the poop. A health issue for our kids," Almira said. Her clothes were those of a life of leisure, but her face looked like she'd spent her all of her sixty-two years in a factory. Ashin thought it was likely just the result of all the scowling she'd done.

He said, "People like you, every time you want something changed, you find some way to tie it to 'safety.' You know that's utter nonsense. For months, your little group has been shrinking the spaces where dogs can play. Please, Almira, find a cause next time that doesn't take from others simply for the sport of seeing if you can." Turning, he nearly collided with Mateo, and the two of them began walking away.

Almira called behind him, "Ashin! Ashin, you can't talk to me that way! This is a matter of safety!"

As they left the park, Mateo asked, "Who is she?"

Ashin said, "Almira Benton." Almira and Ashin had known each other for decades. She had never been a warm, loving person. As long as he had known her, she had looked only for the clouds in the silver linings, was cynical about every plan for improvement, skeptical of every kind gesture, and suspicious of all generosity.

As far as he knew, she didn't have a grateful bone in her body. Almira seemed to have an insatiable need to feel powerful and impactful. She tried running for office, but too many people knew her too well for her to win. Before the dog issue, she had been on many other missions—usually blocking proposed municipal projects. She would study hard in these efforts, learning and memorizing the most minute financial details, the most esoteric, nuanced bits of information, and of course the ultimate worst-case scenarios. If she knew she couldn't stop a project, she tried to reign it in and shrink it at least. She would frame all opponents as ill-informed or dishonest. In all these efforts, she was relentless, and didn't care a bit if it cost her human relationships. She wrote off lost friends as simple, or corrupted by the lies of her opponents. Ashin thought something horrible must have happened to her as a child, that she felt she needed to seek out fights, these serial battles for control. Or maybe she was just born that way.

"Almira and her little troop have been pestering poor Boothby Baxter for months about putting all dogs on leashes," Ashin said.

"That dog on the beach had no leash," Mateo said.

"That'll be next," Ashin said.

"Why don't they like dogs?" Mateo asked.

"They're just people with a lot of resources, but no real purpose in life, so they invent temporary causes. They have nothing against dogs until they decide they do. The majority of people in Paris are fine with the dogs being off-leash, but they don't have the money, free time, and political connections that Almira and her group does. By the time the average person realizes what's happening, something this community has always enjoyed has been taken away from it. Once they exhaust this crusade, they'll select something else to rail against," Ashin said.

Mateo was quiet a moment, and then asked, "Won't people be angry about it?"

"People like Almira don't care. They live for the drama, and think themselves righteous," Ashin said.

"How can someone feel righteous about a dog leash?" Mateo asked.

"It's the only fight they've got," Ashin said.

They both walked quietly, and just before they arrived home, Ashin said only, "It's sad."

When they got to Mateo's driveway, Ashin stopped walking, and watched the boy head for the house. When the front door opened, even before Mateo entered, Ashin thought he heard shouting from within, but Mateo never hesitated and went inside.

8

As he watched out his kitchen window, Ashin spotted Mitch Mitchell walking cautiously into his backyard, and looking around. Ashin walked toward the front of the house, out onto the porch, and waited there until Mitch appeared. He was walking like a cartoon cat burglar, scanning the windows to see if he'd been spotted.

"Hey, Mitch," Ashin said.

Mitch visibly jumped, and clutched his chest.

"I'm not selling. I told you," Ashin said.

Mitch walked around to the front of the porch, but didn't head for the steps. Still standing on the lawn, he said, "Doc, we don't even have to sell. Houses are being bought before anyone sells them."

"What does that mean?" Ashin asked.

"The McDougal house sold this morning. I hadn't even had time to list it yet, and we got buried in offers," Mitch said.

"What do you mean you didn't list it, but got offers?

How'd anyone know it was for sale?" Ashin asked.

"I'm not entirely sure. We signed on to sell it, and this morning I came in to offers on the house! No sign, no ads, no effort to sell the thing," Mitch said.

"Good offers?" Ashin asked.

Mitch took a step forward, and said, "That's the thing, Doc. The McDougal house sold for $550,000."

"What? Why? That should've been at most $325,000," Ashin said.

"We thought $290,000. Of those first bids we got, the winner was $300,000. We let all the bidders know, and we got a second round of bids. Turned into an auction, and by lunchtime, we went above half a million!" Mitch said.

"Is there oil under the house?" Ashin asked.

"I'm telling you," Mitch said.

"I'm not selling," Ashin said.

"Well, at least think about it. As soon as I told Jamie Wold, he told me to sell their house. They weren't planning on selling either, but if people are willing to pay prices like that," Mitch said.

"Jamie's going to sell?" Ashin asked, looking down the street that way.

"Only if the price is right. You don't have to accept an offer, Doc. You put the house up, and just see what happens. You can turn down offers," Mitch said.

Ashin shook his head, and said, "$500,000."

"$550,000" Mitch corrected.

"Well, it's not for sale," Ashin said.

Mitch said, "One block north of here, an unbuildable sliver of land, stuck between two houses, has a 'SOLD' sign posted on it. Not my deal. I didn't even know it was for sale before it sold. Neither abutting landowner bought it. It was some LLC that got it."

"What will they do with it?" Ashin asked.

"Probably sit on it, wait for one of the neighbors to sell their house, and then sell it to the new buyer, marked up of course," Mitch said. "Ideally, both neighbors will sell and then the LLC can start a bidding war between the two new owners."

Ashin asked, "Remember back when people bought a house, because they loved it, because they wanted to live in it? Because they wanted to be part of a community?"

"I do. Things change. Nothing we can do about it," Mitch said.

Ashin said, "Plus, you know, there's your commission."

"Hey, I didn't cause this, but I might as well make a buck," Mitch said.

"This one's not for sale," Ashin said, and he went back into the house. He went to the kitchen, pulled his test kit down from a cupboard, and checked his blood sugar. The little egg-shaped device read, "220."

"Damn," Ashin said. It hadn't even been symptoms of diabetes that had brought him to the doctor, instead it had been a pain just under his ribs. Turned out to be a gall stone, and so he'd had his gall bladder removed. A day surgery, in and out, and so he thought it was no big deal.

When he woke up in the recovery area, a nurse he'd never seen before, came to check his vitals and his IV, and then simply said, "You're a diabetic. You're going to need to take insulin from now on."

Ashin was shocked. He didn't know this nurse, his head wasn't even clear, his doctor wasn't present, and with no warm up to lead him to this new reality… she just dropped it on him cold.

"That's how you're going to tell me? Do you always deliver bad news to strangers as you pass through?" Ashin asked.

"Sir, you have no cause to speak to me that way. It's the truth," the nurse replied.

"Go on, I don't want you doing anything else for me," he said.

She turned and left. He never saw her again. It was about an hour later when his own doctor had come by, and Ashin told him what had happened. That's when his doctor suggested daily walks, and expedited his release.

Ashin looked out the window toward the Funk house. It seemed, with his blood sugar over 200, that he would have to try to walk a bit farther, faster, or more often.

9

Ashin and Mateo headed out for another walk. As they passed what had been the McDougal house, they saw a man, perhaps in his mid-forties, standing in his bathrobe, pajama pants, and slippers. He was pounding a homemade sign into the front lawn.

The sign read, "Keep Off Grass," and it was blocking the entrance of the worn trail that crossed the front yard and led to the beach. The man stepped back into the street, seemingly to evaluate his work, and was surprised by Ashin and Mateo.

"Oh hi!" he said.

"Good morning," Ashin said.

"Do you live in the neighborhood?" the man asked.

"Just there," Ashin said, pointing back at his house.

"Grandson visiting?" the man asked with a smile.

"I'm not his grandson. I'm a neighbor, too. One house over from his," Mateo said.

"Ah. What's your name, son?" the man asked, still smiling.

"Mateo Funk."

The man's face fell a bit, and the smile was a bit less genuine. He said, "Well, nice to meet you. I'm Percy Glerter. My wife, Violet, and I just moved in."

"Ashin Asilomar," Ashin said, extending his hand.

"We moved in not long ago, too," Mateo said.

"Is that right?" Percy asked. "Both of you?"

"Naw, he's been here forever," Mateo said, thumbing at Ashin.

"Well, I can certainly understand why," Percy said, his smile refreshed, "My wife and I love the feel of this town. How neighborly and warm it is," he said, gesturing toward Ashin and Mateo, with smile refreshed, as if they were proof.

Mateo asked, "You're cutting off the path?"

Percy looked over at his new sign, and said, "Oh, well, yeah. I mean, it's not just the damage to the lawn; it's a liability thing. You know, if someone got hurt on my property… well, it's my liability insurance. Can't have someone getting hurt. It's a safety thing, after all."

A woman came out onto the front porch, and then approached. "Hi there! Percy, who's this?" she asked, smiling as broadly as her husband had.

"Hon, this is Asher and Matt, they live just over there. Our neighbors," Percy said.

"I'm Violet," she said, shaking hands with them both.

Mateo coughed.

"We just love Paris, we're so excited to be here. It's perfect. Exactly what we were looking for, to escape. It's so idyllic! Like a small town from a book," Violet said.

"Escape from where?" Mateo asked.

"Colorado," Percy said.

"People usually leave California to move to Colorado," Ashin said.

Violet said, "Oh, not as much anymore. We were in the Springs, and it was so right-wing religious nut-job crazy there. We really wanted to move somewhere people were much more warm, inclusive, accommodating. You know?"

Percy said, "Tolerant. Easy-going and open-minded. You know?"

Ashin nodded, and said, "Well, welcome to Paris." He took a step to continue with the walk.

Mateo only tilted his head, like a confused German Shepherd might, and Percy and Violet chanted a chorus of, "Thank you, thanks, and bye now bye."

Ashin pulled on Mateo's arm, and got him walking. Mateo cleared his throat, surely about to speak, but Ashin shushed him. It would likely be better to be well out of earshot of the Glerters before Mateo began with was sure to be a barrage of questions and observations.

Ashin said, "I know, I know. Just keep walking."

Mateo did look back, over his shoulder, at the little sign. He then walked into Ashin, who stopped and sighed.

Mateo said, "Sorry. The Glerters went back in the house."

Ashin said nothing.

As they took their next steps, Mateo asked, "Don't they…?"

"They have no idea," Ashin said, cutting him off, and the two walked toward the park.

"But if they think things here are perfect, why change…?" Mateo began.

Ashin cut him off again, "Most people say things are 'perfect, except for' and then they try to change the exceptions."

Mateo said, "If there is something to change, then it wasn't perfect."

"People do that all the time. Haven't you ever heard people say things like, 'He's one of my best friends.' There can't be more than one 'best' of anything. Language used to be more useful," Ashin said.

"Weren't you a dentist?" Mateo asked.

"I was, why?" Ashin replied.

"You sound more like a grumpy teacher," Mateo said.

There was a pause before Ashin said, "At my age, Mateo, we're all grumpy teachers."

* * *

Over the coming weeks, more houses sold, and as locals adapted to the sign Percy Glerter had erected, the Glerter lawn was avoided, and folks cut through other neighboring yards. Soon, more little signs appeared, until they lined that side of the road, protecting lawns, as far as the eye could see in either direction.

People were left with few choices on how to get to the beach. Luckily, it turned out, that there was a sliver of municipal property that passed between two residential lots, providing access.

10

Ashin was on his front porch, tightening up his chair, when Mateo came up his front steps. He was wearing swim trunks, flip-flops, and had a towel slung around his neck.

"Hi Mateo, how are we doing?"

"Are we still allowed to go to the beach?" Mateo asked.

"Why?"

"It was crowded. These two guys were asking people if they were locals. They must not have believed me at first, because they asked what neighborhood I live in, how long I've lived there, that stuff," Mateo said.

Ashin's brow furrowed. "That's odd. It's a public beach. The homeowners can only claim to the wrack line, just as we discussed."

"I'm just saying what happened," Mateo said.

"There were a lot of people?" Ashin asked.

"And cars parked on the side of the road near where you go in now," Mateo said.

Ashin scratched his head. "Maybe it was an event,

you know, maybe a birthday party or something."

Mateo shrugged his shoulders.

"Did they ask you to leave?" Ashin asked.

"Nuh-uh," Mateo said.

"Did they ask anyone to leave?"

"Not that I saw," Mateo said. "It was more like they were only taking count, and not doing anything about it."

"Did you hear a lot of people say they weren't local?" Ashin asked.

"Everyone I heard was from here in Paris," Mateo said. "But I wondered if the rules had changed or something."

"Were you there by yourself?" Ashin asked.

Mateo paused and then said, "Unless I'm with you, I'm always by myself."

Ashin felt a wave of sympathy for Mateo. Alone doesn't always mean lonely, but there was something in his voice. "Want me to go for a walk on the beach with you?"

Mateo didn't answer, but instead asked, "What are you working on?"

Ashin looked back down at the chair. "Over time, this thing loosens up, and I have to tighten it."

"With that?" Mateo asked, pointing.

"It's called an Allen key wrench," Ashin said.

"Who was Allen?" Mateo asked.

"I think that was the name of the company who came up with them," Ashin said.

"Why not use regular screws? Why make someone have to buy a special wrench?" Mateo asked.

"People are always trying new things. It's good to be creative and inventive, isn't it?" Ashin asked.

"Only when you make something better. Otherwise, it's a waste of time. Do those hold better than regular screws?" Mateo asked.

"Someone must think so," Ashin said. "And if I have the room to spin the wrench all the way around, it's faster."

"Do you have the room with the chair?" Mateo asked.

"Well, no."

Mateo looked at the porch floor, and then the chair, and then Ashin. He said, "I think it's weird that some guy looked at a screw and thought, 'I can do better than that,' and he believed it was so much better that everyone would buy a new tool to use it. Why not leave some things alone?"

Ashin stood the chair back on its feet, and asked, "Did you eat lunch?"

"I did," Mateo said.

"Well, I haven't. Want to watch me eat?" Ashin asked.

Mateo grinned. "You bet."

11

Mitch Mitchell's vehicle was parked in front of Ashin's house again. Ashin went to the back windows, to see if the real estate agent was prowling around his backyard, but he wasn't there.

Ashin went out onto his front porch in time to see Mitch bear-hugging three signs, all reading, "SOLD." Mitch threw them into the back of his SUV. He clapped his hands clean and then walked toward Ashin's house.

"Hey Doc," Mitch said.

"How are we, Mitch?"

"Doing great," he said.

"Sales are still strong, I see," Ashin said.

"You got that right," Mitch said. "And now there's the proposal for apartments."

"Apartments?" Ashin asked. "That many people want to move here?"

"The town's five-year plan did say they wanted to attract young families with kids. Average age in town just keeps going up," Mitch said.

"Young families would be nice," Ashin said, glancing over at the Funk's house.

"Yeah, this proposed apartment building, it's got thirty apartments, with retail space on the ground floor," Mitch said.

"Mr. Funk next door did say he wanted a coffee shop," Ashin said.

"Who doesn't?" Mitch asked.

"I suppose," Ashin said.

Mitch came up the steps, lowered his voice, and said, "Not only that, some of the folks that sold their homes in Paris... they can't find houses to buy at reasonable prices. Between us, the market is getting a bit out of control. Imagine if you sold your house for $500,000, and then you find out that any house you want to buy costs more than that? You gave up your neighborhood, the house you loved... all that... for nothing? Can be a bitter pill. You might have been right all along, Doc. A bunch of people with half-a-million dollars in the bank, stuck living with relatives in Salinas, thinking that instead of a paid-off house in Paris, they're looking at having a mortgage again, and their pile of cash will just be a down payment. So, maybe some of them could move into the new apartments."

"It's a done deal? The apartments are coming?" Ashin asked.

"Oh no, the first Town Council meeting on it is Thursday. You can still watch them on local cable," Mitch said. "I'm sure they'll be discussing it for a while to come. Planning Board, too, and maybe Zoning Board of Appeals, and there will be public forums, of course.

You know how it is."

Ashin remembered the series of meetings that led to the bulldozing of shops, including his first dentist's office, and the building of a strip-mall that no one likes, all those years before, and all in the name of progress.

Mitch turned, went back down the steps, and said, "Got to run. Have a good day, Doc."

"You too," Ashin said. He watched Mitch climb into his SUV and pull away. As the engine noise faded, Ashin heard shouting. He looked toward the Funk house, couldn't see anyone, but could hear Deepak Funk roaring about something. Ashin couldn't pick out what the man was angry about, but he sounded livid. It was followed by a woman shouting, and then the two voices overlapped. Ashin scanned the dark windows for any sign of Mateo, and hoped the boy wasn't in there.

12

After supper on Thursday, Ashin sat in front of the television he rarely watched, and turned it to the local cable station. Once there, he saw the camera was trained on the empty Town Council seats, with text across the bottom, which read, "TC meeting will begin soon."

Just as the first council member appeared, along with Town Manager Boothby Baxter, there was a knock at Ashin's door. Opening it, he found Mateo standing there.

"Can I come in?" Mateo asked.

"Well, I was just about to watch something," Ashin said.

"What is it?" Mateo asked.

"Local government. You'd probably find it terribly boring," Ashin said.

Mateo looked at his feet, and then back at Ashin, and asked, "Can I come in anyway?"

Ashin looked out the window, toward the Funk

house, and wondered if the boy simply wanted to be somewhere other than home. Ashin opened the screen door, and said, "Come on in, but you have to let me hear the television."

"I won't talk," Mateo said, and headed for the couch.

"Hey," Ashin said.

"Huh?" Mateo asked.

"Shoes," Ashin said, and pointed at a little piece of carpet near the door.

Mateo came back, sat on the floor, and pulled off his sneakers. He placed them on the carpet, and then went to the couch. Ashin sat in his chair.

The Town Council was all in place, with Boothby Baxter sitting to the far left. The camera panned, and there was a pretty woman sitting at a wide wooden table, and behind her were a dozen metal folding chairs, full of people.

The council chairman tapped his gavel, but didn't say anything. It was Boothby Baxter who spoke first, and said, "There's been a change to tonight's agenda. Cyrus Eliason, who was going to appear to present his proposal for a new apartment building and retail space had to postpone until a future meeting, so we will move onto the second item. Shelley Kohan has a proposal for a new business in town. Ms. Kohan?"

"Ah," Ashin said.

"What?" Mateo asked.

"I was tuning in to see the apartment thing," Ashin said.

On the TV, the woman seated at the table, Shelley, said, "Thank you, Mr. Baxter. I have a proposal here, to renovate the former Burger Chief, and open a new business which would sew and sell fine leather products." She walked forward, and handed a copy of her proposal to each councilor and to Boothby Baxter, and then returned to the large table. The folding chairs behind her were largely empty, except for two people who had remained.

"Not a tannery, is it?" one councilor asked.

"No, sir," Shelley said, "We would purchase fine leather, create our artisanal products on site, and sell them from the storefront and online."

The councilor said, "Oh good, those tanneries really smell."

"Leather?" Mateo asked.

"Shhh," Ashin said.

As Shelley presented, Mateo asked, "I thought you were only interested in the apartments."

"I thought you weren't going to talk," Ashin replied.

On the television, Boothby Baxter said, "Thank you, Ms. Kohan. We'll look these over, and refer this to the Planning Board. They'll be in touch."

Mateo coughed.

Shelley, on TV, said, "Thank you, Mr. Baxter."

Mateo coughed again, and again. Ashin turned off the television, and asked, "Catching a cold?"

"No," Mateo said.

"That cough sounds pretty rough," Ashin said.

Mateo stood up and walked to his shoes, started putting them on, and said, "I have cystic fibrosis."

"CF? I haven't noticed a cough before," Ashin said.

"It's later in the day than usual. I just had PT. I cough

more after," Mateo said. "I haven't really been sick. Had sinus surgery once, but I haven't been really sick except when I was a tiny baby. Don't remember it."

"Why didn't you tell me before?" Ashin asked.

"I don't know. We haven't really discussed medical stuff," he said.

"And you're fine on the walks," Ashin said.

"Like I said, I haven't really been sick. I've got like 100 percent lung function. So far," he said, putting on his second shoe.

Ashin asked, "Why are you leaving?"

Mateo stopped, paused, and then said, "I don't know."

"Do your folks know where you are?" Ashin asked.

"Yeah," Mateo said.

"Want to play cards? Or you can help me with my puzzle," Ashin said, pointing to a 1,000-piece puzzle on the small dining table.

Mateo glanced over at the table. "Yeah, okay," he said, taking his shoes off once more.

"We won't finish it. We'll just work on it a bit," Ashin said.

Mateo walked over to the puzzle. "What is it supposed to look like when it's done?" he asked.

"Oh, I put the cover away. I don't look at it," Ashin said.

"But you saw it once," Mateo said. "I've never seen it."

Ashin went to the closet, took out the cover of the puzzle box, showed it to Mateo, and said, "It's Charles Bridge, in Prague." He then returned the cover to the closet. When he returned to the table, he said, "There, now we've both seen it. Let's work on it a bit."

Mateo said nothing, and knelt on a chair, scanning the pieces. He grabbed two, one in each hand, and simultaneously placed them. And then he did it again.

"How are you doing that?" Ashin asked.

"Doing what?" Mateo asked, and blinked twice.

"Nothing, keep going," Ashin said, and the two of them spent the next couple of hours placing pieces. Ashin placed them only one at a time, and half as quickly as Mateo.

13

Walking alone, with a quicker pace and hearing nothing but the earliest birds, Ashin noticed that the telephone poles, as far as he could see were plastered with the same sign. These were hung higher than the FOR SALE and KEEP OUT signs that now stood on so many lawns. He approached the closest one, and read it:

"Notice: As of August 1st, all dogs outside of their own yards and homes must be on a leash at all times. This is in accordance with Chapter 7, Article 1, sec. 7-1-15 of the Paris Municipal Ordinances. —Paris Police Department."

Below this there was a black silhouette of what looked like a Doberman pinscher, without a leash, but with a large red circle around the animal, and a slash across it.

"Almira," Ashin said, shaking his head. In all the decades Ashin had lived in Paris, he had never heard of a single serious dog attack. He felt sorry for the police officers who would now be forced to stop elderly women getting a little air with their older Corgis and

Yorkies, to inform them that the way they had lived for all these years was now against the law. Or maybe the police wouldn't. Ashin was sure that at least a couple of the senior members of the Paris PD would operate on a "nil seen" basis, unless there was a large, aggressive dog, and there actually was a reason to step in.

How far would the anti-dog cohort go? Ashin wondered. Not to mention, they had just installed that fence at Wilson Point. It must have cost the town quite a bit of money to first purchase it, and then to install it. The new ordinance made it meaningless. All the off-leash areas for dogs were gone, and the fence was made obsolete.

All simply exercises in control and politics. When people like Almira didn't get their way with their phone calls, petitions, and emails, they went to court, forcing the town to spend even more money, and tying up precious court time. Ashin thought it was just sad. Looking down, he saw he was standing next to a sign that read, "Private Property. No Trespassing."

He looked back at the poster on the pole. It made him want to go out and get a dog. What would they do? Lock up a retired dentist? He sighed, cut his walk short, and went home.

14

~

There was something sticking out of his mailbox, which Ashin thought odd since he'd already gotten today's mail. Pulling it free, he saw it was a full color flier, featuring a man in a shirt and tie, sleeves rolled back a bit. Above the man's head, in quotes, it read, "Can I buy your house?"

"They're putting those in everyone's mailbox. Even the homes that recently sold."

Ashin turned to the voice, and saw Mitch Mitchell approaching from the street.

Mitch said, "Technically, you can't put just any junk in a mailbox. It's supposed to be for mail."

"Who is he?" Ashin asked.

"Who knows, probably just a model. The agency listed at the bottom is up in San Jose," Mitch said.

Scanning down, Ashin confirmed that the address and phone number was, indeed, from San Jose. "They're coming down into your territory," he said.

"We used to be so much better about that. We tried

to stay in our own hunting grounds," Mitch said. "Too much money at stake now, I guess."

"Must be running out of houses to sell," Ashin said.

"Only making it worse. If you hold an open house these days, people are pulling out checkbooks on the front lawn. I used to walk people through and point out things that needed fixing, but trying to highlight the potential. Now, they cram into the house, don't care about any problems, and I then I end up holding an auction on the steps, with all these folks with their checkbooks open," Mitch said.

"Where's it going to end, Mitch?" Ashin said.

"When we run out of inventory, I suppose. Don't get me wrong, things are good for me. I'll likely retire earlier than planned, but the warmth of selling a nice couple a family home… those days seem gone. Now, it's much more like feeding seagulls," Mitch said.

Ashin looked down the road at the signs that had changed the look and feel of the neighborhood. *Seagulls*, he thought. Then, near the limit of where Ashin could see, men were working in a front yard.

"A fence," Ashin said. "They're putting up a fence."

Mitch looked that way, and said, "Ah, yeah. I saw that driving up. Too bad."

"It is," Ashin said.

Mitch cleared his throat, and said, "Well, gotta go sell more houses."

Ashin watched him head for his SUV, and then looked once more in the direction of the fence installation.

15

Mateo and Ashin walked single file for a bit before Mateo stepped off the sidewalk, turned, and stopped. "Are we going to the park?" he asked.

"Let's go to the carousel," Ashin said.

"Cool, we haven't walked there," Mateo said.

Ashin asked, "Have your parents taken you yet?"

Mateo said nothing, but began walking again, and they were side-by-side. He pointed, and said, "Hey, a fence."

"I saw them putting it up," Ashin said.

When they reached it, they stopped, and Mateo read the orange sign with black lettering, "STAY OUT. Trespassers will be prosecuted. Under video surveillance."

"Wow, what do they have in there?" Mateo asked.

"What do you mean?" Ashin asked.

"I mean, what are they protecting in there? You think it's a lot of money, or gold, or something?" Mateo asked.

Ashin looked at the house, and said, "I don't think

they're trying to protect something valuable in there. I think they're trying to keep everybody else out."

"Like, they're hiding?" Mateo asked.

"Sort of," Ashin said. "Or maybe they're just territorial."

"Weird," Mateo said.

Ashin thought it amusing that Mateo, of all people, would call others weird, but he was right. It was strange. Normally, when an animal is territorial, it marks off an area and claims it because of the resources in the territory that will sustain it. Wolves claim a hunting area, so that the pack will have food. Or animals will claim an area for exclusivity of mating. These people snapping up quarter-acre lots, and marking them with chain-link, weren't doing that. They weren't keeping competitive suitors away from their mates, and they weren't protecting the bounty of acorns falling from the oaks.

So maybe it was fear, Ashin thought. *Fear of everything.*

"Come on, let's go," Mateo said.

When the carousel building came into view, they could also see the Pacific Ocean. It was relatively calm in the bay that day. The building was large, nearly windowless on the east side, with narrow clapboard siding, painted white.

"What's this place?" Mateo asked as they came around the corner and approached the door.

"The carousel is in here," Ashin said.

"It's inside? Don't they usually have a roof right on them?" Mateo asked.

Ashin held the door, and then followed the boy inside.

The overpowering scent of candy makers met them, and the music from the immense carousel was loud. It was in perfect condition, with bright colors. Wooden horses galloped in a circle, rising and falling on brass poles. The center was mirrored, and there were brass rings hanging from hooks about the horses.

"Wow! How many horses are there?" Mateo asked.

"More than seventy," Ashin said. "This carousel was here when I was a little boy. It's more than 100 years old. The horses are hand-carved."

"It's the same horses?" Mateo asked.

"I think so. They repair them, and repaint them, but I've never heard of them replacing horses," Ashin said.

"Cool," Mateo said.

"Want to ride on it?" Ashin asked. The carousel was mostly empty, but a horse did come by with a man standing beside what looked like his five-year-old daughter, grinning and riding.

Mateo said, "I think I'm too old, but maybe."

Ashin nodded, and said, "This evening, most of the horses will be taken, and people will be walking all around here. It gets busy later, after dinner."

Mateo asked, "Are those all candy shops?" He was pointing down the aisle that ran along one side of the carousel.

It had all been designed to look like a street from 1910, with a carousel on one side, and a series of shops on the other. Over the decades, most of the shops had become artisanal confectionaries.

"Want some cotton candy?" Ashin asked.

"What's that's place?" Mateo asked.

It certainly wasn't a candy store. Above the wooden door and the plate glass window was a sign that read, "Magnani Records."

"A record shop?" Ashin asked, not remembering this business being here.

"There are no records in there," Mateo said.

Looking in through the four-foot window, Ashin could see the boy was right. Not a single product on the lone shelf. There was a counter, behind which stood an elderly man, and to one side there was a large booth. On the wooden side of the booth was ancient lettering which read, "Hear your voice as others hear you! Record your own voice! 50 cents!"

The elderly man behind the counter was looking back at them now, not moving.

"Anyone can record themselves at home now," Mateo said.

"Fifty cents was probably a lot of money when that was painted. People would live their whole lives having never heard their own recorded voices," Ashin said.

"Want to go look?" Mateo said.

"Sure," Ashin said, and smiled.

As they entered, the man behind the counter said, "Good day, folks."

"Good day," Ashin replied, and he followed Mateo to the booth.

"Are you Mr. Magnani?" Mateo asked.

"Nope," the man said, and nothing else.

When Mateo looked at Ashin, he only shrugged.

"Can I look inside?" Mateo asked.

"Of course, go on in," the man said.

Ashin smiled at the man, appreciatively, and he nodded back.

Mateo stepped in, and Ashin could see the boy nearly filled the small space, before stepping back out. Looking at the man, Mateo asked, "So, people talk and the booth records them?"

"Most folks sing. They sing their favorite song, and then they leave with a record. An honest-to-God record. You ever seen a record, boy?" the man asked.

"Like for a record player? I've seen them. This booth makes them?" Mateo asked.

"Wax?" Ashin asked.

"Vinyl. Straight to vinyl," the man said.

"Is that right?" Ashin asked, and looked back at the booth.

"Six inches. About three minutes of singing," the man said.

"I bet it's not fifty cents anymore," Ashin said, and chuckled.

"Afraid not. The vinyl blanks that it uses cost about $4 apiece. So, I charge $6 per record," the elderly man said.

"Very reasonable," Ashin said.

"Can I sing?" Mateo asked.

"What?" Ashin asked.

"Can I make a record? Will you lend me the $6?" Mateo asked.

"You sing?" Ashin asked.

"If I couldn't, I wouldn't ask," Mateo said, his eyebrows furrowed.

"You don't have a guitar or anything," the elderly man said.

"I'll go *a capella*," Mateo said, and then looked at Ashin.

"Okay, I'll spot you," Ashin said, and pulled a $10 bill from his pocket.

"You got a way to play it at home?" the elderly man asked.

"I've got a phonograph," Ashin said.

"A what?" Mateo asked.

"A record player," Ashin said.

"What will you sing?" the man asked, coming around the corner, and opening a panel on the side of the recording booth.

"I learned it in Texas, from this lady, but I can't sing it as sad as it should be," Mateo said.

"You're too young. You need more practice at being sad," the man said.

"I think I've had plenty of practice," Mateo said.

The man said, "Step inside. See these numbers here? 1-8-0? Those will countdown to the end of the record. When it says 0, you've run out of time. You got that?"

Mateo nodded and cleared his throat, and then closed the door.

"Is it soundproof?" Ashin asked, looking in through the small window.

Mateo shook his head "no."

"It's not, but almost," the old man said, "When he gets going, we should try to be quiet for three minutes."

Ashin nodded.

The man stood in front of the door, looking in through the window, and said, "Okay, in 3 seconds. 3, 2, 1, go!" He flipped a switch on the outside of the booth.

Both men could faintly hear Mateo sing. He was swaying, and sometimes closing his eyes. Ashin couldn't make out the lyrics, but it seemed the boy might have a nice enough voice. After three minutes, the session was over.

"It'll be ready in a minute," the older man said as Mateo exited the booth.

"Was that fun?" Ashin asked.

Mateo shrugged, and said, "Yeah. Thanks."

The old man tried to give Ashin his $4 in change, but Ashin waved him off, saying, "Keep it."

"Thank you, sir," the elderly man said, "And here is your record." He handed Mateo the new vinyl record in a paper sleeve. Mateo didn't take it, and said, "Give it to him. He paid for it."

Ashin took the record, and said, "You really can have it."

"If I want to listen, I can come to your place," Mateo said.

Thanking the elderly man, they left. Ashin carried the little record, and Mateo trailed a bit. Ashin asked, "So, who was it that sang it in Texas?"

"Just a neighbor, but she was nice. She was like a mom to my mother, and my mother needed that," Mateo said.

Ashin asked, "And she used to sing?"

"All the time," Mateo said.

As they passed the new chain link fence, with the new sign, Mateo shook his head.

Ashin said, "There are no neighbors anymore. Not like that lady in Texas."

"You're like that," Mateo said.

Ashin said, "Thanks. You're a pretty good neighbor, too."

"Really?" Mateo asked.

"Really," Ashin said.

Mateo grinned, and peeled off, crossing the street, and said, "See you tomorrow!"

Ashin crossed his lawn, and carried the new record into his house. He slipped off his shoes, and put the record down. Ashin washed his hands, came back to the record player, and removed the potted plant from its lid. Pulling the little record from the paper sleeve, he examined it. No printing on the label, the grooves shiny in the light. He placed it on the turntable, it began to spin, and Ashin carefully placed the needle.

Although the recording was a bit scratchy, Ashin listened as Mateo's voice filled the living room.

"One tent ain't better than the others around
But everyone feels that the others have found
A safer place to keep the secret they share
You can move your tent, but you're always right there.

Oh, wishing and dreaming is fun when you're young
But soon it's a tally of what you ain't done
Your memories are joys to share at the end
Hard, though, to carry if you haven't a friend."

Ashin was impressed, the voice was sweet, but then, it grew louder, and more powerful.

"She powders the white, and accents with the red

She paints on the black, so they know she ain't dead
She wants pretty horses, gets monkeys instead
She's a poet in a circus, who's trapped in her head."

Ashin lifted the needle, with the song only half-sung. He turned off the record player, and closed the lid, leaving Mateo's song on the turntable. Ashin looked out his window toward the Funk house. The kid had a lot of layers, and yet they rarely got past the small talk. *Maybe small talk is what the boy is missing,* Ashin thought. Looking down at the record player, Ashin said, "He's certainly older than he should be."

16

~

"I don't know about going back to that beach. They were asking everyone if they're local, remember?" Mateo said.

"But you are local now," Ashin said, and they headed out.

Mateo had a towel around his neck. "I know but they seemed protective of their beach," he said.

"Well, below the wrack line…" Ashin said.

Mateo stopped walking, and said, "Please never say 'wrack line' again. You keep saying that. The rules don't matter to some people."

Ashin said nothing, but he wondered how often he had said "wrack line." He knew Mateo was right. The rules don't matter to some people, and especially not to some of those who have more money or connections than their neighbors.

Mateo asked, "Did you listen to me singing on the record?"

"Some of it. I think you sing very well," Ashin said. "Sounded almost like a country song."

"More like Appalachian folk, maybe old-time," Mateo said.

"You've studied music?" Ashin asked.

"I read about it,' Mateo said.

Ashin sniffed. "I didn't think anyone your age read anymore."

"I wish there were more people my age around here," Mateo said.

"Would you read less? Do you read because you're bored or lonely?" Ashin asked.

Mateo stepped off the sidewalk, and then back on. "I read because I love to, but maybe also because I always have. When I was in Texas, I had friends. We used to read together, on the carpet. Just lying there with books, reading, on rainy afternoons. We were given books, but not like how some people hand a kid a mop. They didn't give us books like they were a necessary chore to get done. They didn't give us sad books and say, 'Go read this, it's a classic.' We were given books, and time, to read in the same way we were given toys to play with. They didn't give us books that made people feel worse about themselves and world around them. It was exciting to get a new book; they were adventures."

Ashin thought the boy was remarkably insightful, and said, "You have books here, right?"

"I have time to think, too," Mateo said. "All I'm missing are some friends."

"When school starts, you'll make some friends," Ashin said.

"I don't know. This place is becoming all fences and angry signs," Mateo said.

"Do you talk to your Texas friends? On the phone?" Ashin asked.

Mateo said only, "No."

Ashin left it alone, and felt bad for the kid.

After going the long way around, and crossing the municipal land to access the beach, Ashin saw people on the sand. About half of them packing up and leaving.

One lady passed them, her blanket rumpled in her arms, and as she went by she said, "Watch out for the beach Nazis."

Ashin and Mateo went to about mid-beach, and Mateo spread his towel. The boy sat on it, but Ashin remained on his feet when he saw two men, in their 50s, approaching. One had a sheet of paper in his hand.

"Hey there," that man said. "I'm Davy Silvio, and this is Chuy Lopez."

"I know who you are. I'm Ashin Asilomar. I repaired your chipped front teeth when you were a kid," Ashin said.

"Oh right! Hey Dr. Asilomar, how are you?" Davy said, and then he ran his tongue over his front teeth.

"Fine, fine. Thanks. What's this all about?" Ashin asked.

"Well, the beaches have been getting crowded lately, so much so that people who live here can't get on them without being shoulder to shoulder with outsiders," Davy said.

"We've been coming here since before I can remember, and we used to have these beaches just to ourselves. You know, with people actually from Paris," Chuy said.

"Well, you know I'm from Paris," Ashin said.

"We do. And let me check to see if your address is on the list. See, access to the beach isn't just for people who live right on the beach," Davy said.

Ashin exhaled, relieved. At least he seemed to know the public had a right to be here.

"No, there are some properties that are not on the beach, but they have deeded access to the beach, even a block or two away," Davy said.

"Deeded access?" Mateo asked.

"Written in the deed, the people who own the property have the legal right to come here," Chuy said.

"What is your address, Dr. Asilomar?" Davy said, his voice friendly.

"The United States of America," Ashin said.

"Huh?"

"Every bit of this beach that is underwater at high tide is owned by the State of California, and is therefore public. No one can chase people off of it. The public has the right to fish there, swim there, walk there. It doesn't matter what a deed says, or what your list says," Ashin said.

"Technically, that might be true," Chuy said.

"It's true in every way," Ashin said.

"Now look, our families have been here for decades," Davy said.

"I know that. I remember a lot of their teeth. I also know your father would not approve of what you're doing," Ashin said.

Davy's face darkened. "Maybe, you and the kid should just go."

"Call a cop," Ashin said. "They'll tell you what I just

told you. This is a public beach. We'll leave before high tide drives us onto that private land up there."

"We're just trying to keep things like they were," Davy said.

"If that's true, go tear down all the signs and fences. Let kids cross the lawns, and come onto the beaches without being harassed. Act neighborly," Ashin said.

"Listen here," Davy said, and took a step closer to Ashin.

Chuy intervened, and said, "Hey man, just let him and the kid stay. Don't let them ruin our day."

"Ruin your day? Are you having fun?" Mateo said.

"Shut up," Davy said.

"Come on, let's go," Chuy said.

At Chuy's insistence, Davy turned, and the two men walked away, with the list held low. *It's as if it had been a game*, Ashin thought, *and that I spoiled it.*

"We should just leave," Mateo said.

"What? After all that in order stay?" Ashin asked.

"That's the point. Those guys made the day feel bad, and they made the beach feel bad. Some people can stay, some people can't. It makes the beach gross," Mateo said.

Ashin shook his head. "It's up to you, but don't you think that if we leave, we are letting them win?"

Mateo stood up and said, "Feels like they already did."

17

Ashin turned on his television. Once again, the camera was trained on empty chairs, with a promise that the Town Council meeting would soon begin. As he sat in the quiet, a soft breeze coming in through the window ruffled the newspapers on his coffee table, and then Ashin heard shouting.

It was coming from next door, and Ashin could hear Deepak and June Funk yelling at each other. He immediately worried about Mateo. Was he home? Was he in the middle of the fighting? Ashin wished he couldn't make out any of the words.

"You can't blame any of this on me!" June Funk shouted.

"It's not all in my head!" Deepak shouted back.

"It's always only in your head!" June said.

"I'm not crazy!" Deepak said. "I won't let you mix me up!"

"Look at what happened in Texas! Talk about gas lighting!" June said.

“That was ruled an accident!” Deepak said.

Ashin got to his feet, closed his window, and scanned for any sign of Mateo. There was none, and so he returned to the TV. After sheets of paper were passed around by the council, signed by each member in turn, Boothby Baxter opened the meeting by introducing Almira Benton, and the agenda item.

“The issue of dogs and safety in Paris,” he said.

Almira, standing and facing the council, said, “That’s right. As you know, we have had issues with dogs in Paris for some time, but now with all these people moving in with their dogs, it’s worse than ever.”

Boothby Baxter said, “All dogs should be on leash, except in the fenced area at the park.”

Almira said, “Well, yes, but as it turns out, even dogs on leashes poop everywhere. And no one cleans up after their dogs. I propose that the town provide personnel to mark each pile of dog feces with a small marker, perhaps a little flag, to make it clear to the townspeople how serious the problem is. When people look out at a field, and they see all these little flags, then they’ll understand.”

There were groans and chuckles from the audience.

She turned back, and said, “It is a real safety issue!”

Boothby Baxter cleared his throat, and asked, “You’re proposing that we send town employees out to mark dog excrement?”

“That’s exactly what I’m proposing,” she said.

A councilor asked, “Are you serious? You want us to use taxpayer money to create a ‘poop patrol’ and mark dog shit with flags? You can’t see how ridiculous that is?

What a waste of time, labor, and money that is?"

Almira was taken aback, and then said, "You clearly don't understand how dangerous this filth is. It's a safety issue."

Watching his television, Ashin groaned at the words "safety issue."

Boothby Baxter said, "You know that town employees work all day. We don't have a bunch of workers sitting around, hoping something will come up. If they do what you suggest, they would have to stop doing other work. Unless you are proposing we hire a poop patrol?"

Almira said, "Stop calling it that. This is just as important as anything else they might be doing. And they could empty the garbage can at the park, too. It's always overflowing with dog waste bags."

A councilor asked, "If no one picks up after their dogs, how can the garbage can be full?"

Almira's face darkened, and then she said, "It's not just a hygienic threat either. A dog the other day, on leash, pulled away from its owner and attacked a woman, and she ended up with a black eye."

A councilor asked, "How does a dog give someone a black eye?"

A woman in the audience began speaking, the camera swung that way, and Ashin could see it was Shelley Kohan. She said, "The woman was walking a tiny dog, and Mrs. Green's big goofy lab, Rufus, was excited to meet it. The lab broke away from Mrs. Green, and he ran toward the woman and her little dog. The woman snatched her pup, turned, and ran. As soon as she took off, Rufus stopped, but as she went, she looked back over her shoulder, and ran into one of the new ‘No Trespassing’ signs springing up all over town. That’s how she got that shiner.”

A couple councilors and some of the audience members snickered.

Shelley shrugged and said, “Yeah. She was from away.”

More snickers.

“It is not funny. A woman was hurt,” Almira said.

“Those signs and fences are something we should probably get on the agenda,” one of the councilors said.

“Alright,” said Boothby Baxter, and he made a note.

“So, can we expect to see some action on the dog waste?” Almira asked.

“The council will consider it,” Boothby Baxter said.

More snickers. Almira headed toward the back of the room, but never stopped, and walked right out of the building.

“Right,” Boothby Baxter said, “Next on the agenda is Cyrus Eliason, with a proposal for a new apartment building. Mr. Eliason.”

A man in a nice suit, perhaps almost sixty years old, approached and addressed the council. “Thank you for this opportunity. I’d like to share our vision for new housing in Paris. As you know, houses have become prohibitively expensive for most, and there is a shortage of rental homes here. The demand is intense,” Eliason said.

“Where do you want to build it?” a councilor asked.

“There are a couple of possibilities, but the leading contender would be the vacant lot on Sea Foam Street,” Eliason said.

"Where McMurphy's Hardware was," Boothby Baxter said.

"It'd be nice to see something go in there," a councilor said.

"How many units?" another asked.

Eliason said, "We're proposing thirty one-bedroom units."

There was a pause, and then a councilor asked, "How many two-bedroom, three-bedroom?"

Eliason said, "We're proposing only one-bedroom units."

"Why?" a councilor asked.

"We've run the numbers, and for us to recoup our investment, one-bedroom units are the way to go," Eliason said.

A councilor said, "But one of our goals is to attract young families, with children. The idea was not to turn Paris into a retirement community."

Eliason said, "Perhaps we should be careful about judging people."

Boothby Baxter asked, "What do you mean?"

"We shouldn't decide for others that they cannot raise a young family in a one-bedroom apartment," Eliason said.

There was a moment of silence, and then there were snickers from the audience again.

"Where would the kids sleep?" a councilor asked.

"I'm just saying we should be careful not to appear elitist, deciding for others what their family needs," Eliason said.

Boothby Baxter cleared his throat again, and looking

down, he said, "Mr. Eliason, I see we're scheduled for a workshop on this for next Wednesday. And you'll have plans, more details, etc. Is that right?"

Eliason said, "That's right. Looking forward to it."

Boothby Baxter said, "Thank you."

Eliason turned, picked up a bag he hadn't opened, and left.

Ashin stood, turned the television off, and went out onto his front porch. There was no more shouting coming from the Funk's. He sat, closed his eyes, and listened to the quiet.

18

The next morning, Ashin was sweeping the walkway from his front porch to the sidewalk when June Funk and Violet Glerter came by, walking together.

"Good morning," Violet said, and June smiled.

"Morning," Ashin replied.

"Sweeping your walk?" June asked.

Ashin often wondered why people asked questions like that. "Should be a nice day," he said.

"Maybe you could get Mateo out of the house for a walk today," June said, "He's been doing nothing but playing those games for days."

Ashin remembered the fighting he overheard the night before, and winced at the idea of Mateo, playing video games and even with headphones on hearing his parents shout at each other in the next room. "A boy should get some fresh air," he said.

"Did you hear what happened at the Town Council meeting last night?" Violet asked.

"I watched most of it. One-bedroom apartments,"

Ashin said.

"No, I mean the leather shop," Violet said.

"Ah right, they mentioned that in a previous meeting," Ashin said.

"Shelley Kohan wants to open a leather shop," Violet said.

Ashin said, "Yes, I heard," and wondered how these new arrivals could be so plugged in already, and even know a long-time local like Shelley Kohan.

June said, "Is the council always so strict about letting new business in?"

"What happened?" Ashin asked, "I turned it off after the apartment issue."

"Oh, well, Shelley got up and explained her idea, for a little shop, producing and selling fine leather products," June said.

"Which would be lovely," Violet said.

"But the Town Council wanted specifics," June said.

"On the types of leather," Violet said.

"And sources. They were asking, 'Will it be Italian leather? Or Argentine?" June said.

"And 'Maybe American too? Or at least Canadian?' And then the code enforcement officer got involved," Violet said.

"Asking about proposed changes to the building, and about parking," June said.

"But not just how many cars. He was also asking about the parking lot surface, and coats of pavement," Violet said.

"Coats of pavement?" Ashin asked.

"That's right," June said.

"Why did a local Town Council care about the sources of the leather?" Ashin asked.

The women looked at each other, and then June replied, "They didn't say."

"So, Shelley has to come back with a report answering all the questions at the next meeting," Violet said.

"That's right," June said again, "and they told her they'd likely have additional questions forwarded to her as well."

Ashin said, "I missed that part."

"So, is it usually that difficult to open a new business in Paris?" Violet asked.

"It's been so long since someone tried, I honestly don't remember," Ashin said.

"All the more reason they should let Shelley do it. Bring new jobs to town," June said.

Ashin wasn't sure how many jobs Shelley might create with a small leather goods shop, but he let it go.

"This town could use a boost. Many of us moving in are surprised at the number of shops that are vacant, or lots that are empty," Violet said.

"We don't need chain fast food restaurants, though," June said.

"Oh no, we don't need that. Restaurants, sure, but nothing with a drive-through window," Violet said.

"Right," June said.

A single fast food restaurant would likely create fifty jobs, Ashin thought, but said nothing.

There was a pause, and the three of them stood there for a moment, before June asked, "Well, should we continue our little stroll?"

Both women chuckled, and Violet said, “We’ll leave you to your sweeping.”

“Have a nice day,” June said.

“You too,” Ashin said, and then added, “I’ll come see if Mateo is up for a walk in a little while.”

“I’ll let him know,” June said, over her shoulder, as they walked down the fence-and-sign lined street.

Ashin swept the last three feet of walk, and headed back to the house.

19

The newspaper headline read, "All dogs banned, lawsuit forces council's hand" and beneath was a photo of a child's stuffed animal— perhaps a Siberian husky.

"What now?" Ashin asked, as he sat at the kitchen table, and took a sip of coffee. There was no longer any sugar in any of his morning coffee, and he missed it, but the walks were just barely keeping his blood sugar levels where they needed to be.

The story reported that Almira Benton had filed suit against the town, on the issue of dogs, even dogs on leashes, claiming that they represented a health hazard around the town. Boothby Baxter was quoted as saying that while the town thought they could win in court on the merits of the case, the process would likely cost taxpayers in excess of $100,000, especially if Almira appealed upon losing. Boothby Baxter said the council felt the time, money, and effort could be better spent elsewhere. So, the council ruled that all dog owners were to keep their dogs on their own premises, with the only exceptions being when seeking veterinary care, or to drive, with said dogs, outside the town limits of Paris, perhaps to go for a walk. He said that the fencing the town had already purchased, at Almira's insistence, for the off-leash area at the park could be repurposed.

"There's always a need for more fencing," Ashin said to himself.

The story continued on to the issue of emotional support animals. Almira said she had anticipated this, and had a statement from a local therapist, who happened to be her brother-in-law, that the same level of emotional support could be obtained simply by getting a "stuffy"... a furry, stuffed toy dog, of whatever breed a person would like.

The new ordinance carried a fine of $100 for the first offense, and a $250 for subsequent offenses.

"We've lost our minds," Ashin said softly.

There was a knock at the door. He rose to answer it, and found Mateo standing on his porch.

"Ready for a walk?" Ashin asked.

Mateo nodded.

"Be right out," Ashin said. He walked back to the table, took a long swig of coffee, and poured the last third of the mug into the sink. He then joined Mateo on the porch, and asked, "Where do you want to walk to today?"

"Let's not walk to anywhere. Let's just walk," Mateo said.

"Are you okay?" Ashin asked.

"It's a bit tougher to breathe today," Mateo said.

"Should you see your doctor?" Ashin asked.

"My mom called them. My CF doctor is out today,

he'll be back tomorrow. They said if it gets really bad, to go to the emergency room," Mateo said. "I'll be okay. I want to walk."

"We can do that, but don't hide anything. If you start feeling worse, you tell me right away," Ashin said.

"I will," Mateo said. "I'll be fine."

They headed down the street, lined with fences, and it seemed everyone was out working on their own. It appeared they were reinforcing them.

"How is everything else going?" Ashin asked.

"Fine," Mateo said.

Ashin heard nothing but sadness in the boy's voice, and he wondered if the kid was worried about his condition, or if it was loneliness. "You don't sound fine, Mateo," Ashin said.

Mateo walked, staring at the sidewalk, and said, "My parents have been fighting a lot."

"Oh," Ashin said. "Well, moving to a new town can be stressful."

"They've always fought," Mateo said.

Ashin cautiously asked, "Do they hit each other? Or you?"

Mateo looked up at Ashin, and then back at the sidewalk, "They never hit me or each other, but they throw things sometimes."

"I'm sorry, that sounds hard," Ashin said.

"What's hard is my dad is moving out. He's getting an apartment across town," Mateo said.

"Oh, I'm sorry," Ashin said, and then he thought of the proposal for new one-bedroom apartments. Deepak Funk was lucky to find something.

"It's better this way, except on weekends sometimes, I have to go stay with him," Mateo said.

"Don't you want to see your father?" Ashin asked.

"I like spending time with him, but I won't be here for our walks those weekends. And it kind of feels like I'm moving again, even though I'm not. I'd like to get used to a place, and then not leave until I say I want to go," Mateo said. He was gasping a bit as he finished.

"Are you okay?" Ashin asked.

"Yeah, it was just a lot to say while I'm walking," Mateo said. "I'll be with my dad this coming weekend."

"Why does it have to be weekends? School hasn't started," Ashin asked.

"They want to set up a routine, I guess. My mom likes predictability," Mateo said.

"Has she written an algorithm for your visits?" Ashin said.

Mateo looked up at him, brow furrowed, and said, "No."

They walked the basic loop, avoiding the beach, the carousel, the park, and really only saw fences and signs.

"Can I ask how you came to be named Mateo?" Ashin asked.

"My parents named me that," Mateo said.

"That much I assumed. But do you know why they chose it?" Ashin asked.

"You're asking because I'm not Latino, but I have a Spanish name?" Mateo asked.

"I guess so, yeah," Ashin said.

"My father's parents were Canadians living in India, so they named him Deepak. He's not Indian, and doesn't really remember living there," Mateo said.

"And?"

"And, I guess when I was born in Texas, the old man next door had a cute Chihuahua named Mateo, and my parents liked the name," Mateo said.

"You're named after a dog?" Ashin asked.

"Actually, I think the dog and I are named after a saint," Mateo said.

The conversation moved on to small talk about nothing in particular—they didn't talk about the coming school year, nor CF, nor Mateo's family. When they got back to Ashin's house, they were met by a young couple, who seemed excited.

"Do you live here?" the man asked.

"I do," said Ashin.

"It's lovely," said the woman.

"Thank you," Ashin said.

Mitch Mitchell pulled up, almost screeching to a halt. He jumped out of the SUV and started hustling toward them.

The man said, "We'd like to offer you $1.2 million for your house."

"What?" Ashin asked.

"One-point-two," the man said.

"Hold on there," Mitch said.

"It's not worth anything like that. That might be double the actual value," Ashin said.

"Oh, we think it's worth that," the woman said.

"These people are cutting us out, Doc. People running around with their checkbooks, cutting realtors out," Mitch said.

"Wouldn't you need someone to help you with all the paperwork? Help set up financing and inspections, etc.?" Ashin asked.

The man said, "Oh no, we don't need an inspection."

"No contingencies," the woman said, and grinned.

"But for all you know, there's no floor in the place," Ashin said.

"Sounds crooked, doesn't it?" Mitch asked.

The woman said, "Oh, I'm sure it's fine. Besides we just bought another house, on the other end of town, and there was a hole in the roof! You could see the sky! Hardwood floor was ruined, but it was still a steal."

"Stealing alright," Mitch said.

"Why do you need another house?" Mateo asked.

"Need?" the woman asked, seemingly confused by the question.

"And financing isn't an issue, we'll pay in cash if you like. By the end of the day," the man said.

Mitch said, "Don't let them do this. We go way back."

Ashin looked from the man, to the woman, to Mitch, and then Mateo, who shrugged.

"I'm afraid the house isn't for sale," Ashin said.

"$1.5 million," the man said.

"Sorry, I'm going to pass," Ashin said.

"Now he's just being stubborn," the woman said, no longer smiling.

"How much *do* you want?" the man asked. He was shifting his weight from foot to foot.

Mateo said, "He doesn't want to sell it."

"I wasn't talking to you," the man said to Mateo.

"I'm going to ask you to leave," Ashin said, pointing

down the walk and toward the street.

"What, you don't believe in capitalism?" she asked.

"Communist," the man said.

"You heard him, move along," Mitch said.

"We'll simply buy the next house," she said, and looked over at the Funk house.

"You can't buy that house! We just moved in!" Mateo said.

"If you do, you'll have a communist as a neighbor," Ashin said.

"A good fence can fix that," the man said.

"Better make it soundproof. We hold our Karl Marx rallies once a month. They get pretty rowdy," Ashin said.

Mitch snickered.

The man put his arm around the woman, and said, "Let's go. They're crazy. There are plenty of other houses in Paris."

"You'd have better luck in Paris, France," Mitch said.

"Have a nice day," Ashin said.

The couple walked away, muttering something Ashin couldn't hear.

20

Ashin carried his morning coffee onto his front porch and found Mateo sitting out there.

"I thought you were spending this weekend with your father," Ashin said.

"I was, but I asked my mom to come get me. It was getting too weird over there. He was filling sandbags out of the sandbox behind the apartments, you know meant for kids to play in? And then he was carrying them, two at a time, back to the apartment. He's trying to line the inside of the walls with sandbags," Mateo said.

"Did you tell your mother this?" Ashin asked.

Mateo said, "Mom said she'll tell the police. Is he breaking the law?"

"I guess he's stealing sand, but I think mostly they'll just want to check on his state of mind. He's not planning an armed standoff with police or anything? Does he have guns?" Ashin asked.

Mateo looked away and said, "He hasn't been allowed to own guns since Texas."

Ashin took a sip of his coffee and asked, "Do you want to tell me about what happened there?"

Mateo said, "My dad was under a lot of stress, and he's always been… different."

"Was he a reporter there, too?" Ashin asked.

"Too? He hasn't really worked since we've been here. He calls himself 'freelance' now but I don't think he's written anything. But he was a reporter in Texas. He used to write four or five stories each week, but then it was two, and then at the end it was the same story, every week. He became obsessed with writing about corruption in town. He claimed to have proof that the Town Council, the school board, local business owners, every town employee, the local hospital staff, the mailman, almost everyone except our family, was in on some giant conspiracy," Mateo said.

"What sort of conspiracy?" Ashin asked.

"It kept changing. At the end, we weren't allowed to even drink the tap water, because he was sure it was being drugged," Mateo said.

"Then what happened?"

"His boss, a nice editor lady named Marta, told him that they couldn't keep running his stories," Mateo said.

Ashin asked, "So, then he thought she was in on the conspiracy?"

Mateo nodded, and said, "Trying to shut him up."

"Did anyone refer him for psychiatric help?" Ashin asked.

"Mom tried to get him to go see someone, but he refused. It wasn't until the fire that they took him away," Mateo said.

"Was he trying to hurt people with the fire?" Ashin asked.

"The only thing he burned down was our garage. When the fire department arrived, he tried to stop them from putting out the fire. Two cops grabbed him when he started attacking the big fire hose with a rake," Mateo said.

Ashin didn't say anything for a moment, unsure if he should pursue this any further, but then asked, "How did your father come to live with you again?"

"After a couple months, they said he was okay to come home. While he was gone, my mom put the house up for sale. I was surprised it sold with a burned down garage, but it did. She told us we were moving to California. When my dad got out, we were packing. He was very calm, and friendly, and he asked my mom really nicely, in front of us kids, if he could come, too. And at first, he seemed fine," Mateo said.

"What happened?" Ashin asked.

"I'm not sure, but it's like the more those fences and signs went up in the neighborhood, the more anxious he got, and then he stopped taking his medications. He said they weren't doing anything anyway," Mateo said.

"And your parents started fighting?" Ashin asked.

"My mom said he wasn't following their agreement, whatever that was," Mateo said, "And now he's turning his apartment into a bunker. So, I asked my mom to come get me, and then I came over and sat on your porch."

Ashin took another sip of coffee, and said, "You can sit on my porch any time you like, Mateo. Next time, if you want, you can knock on the door and let me know you're out here."

"I've been here since 4:30 a.m.," Mateo said.

"You can especially knock at 4:30 a.m.," Ashin said.

Mateo looked up at Ashin, but didn't saying anything.

"After my coffee, want to go for a walk?" Ashin asked.

Mateo nodded, but still didn't say a word.

21

As Ashin and Mateo made their way toward the park, the sun not yet high enough in the sky to make their way bright, they noticed things were different. When they turned the first corner, the change was even more dramatic.

"Whoa," was all Mateo said.

"Good grief," Ashin replied, "They're really overdoing it now."

The fences, once three or four feet high, had been replaced. They stood twice as tall as Ashin, with signs hanging every six feet, warning of surveillance cameras and instructing that the fence must not be touched.

"What is that on top of the fence?" Mateo asked.

"Razor wire," Ashin said. The taller fencing ran all the way down the street, each lot having met the call of the ongoing effort, the length of it topped with razor-sharp concertina wire.

"Is the fence electrified?" Mateo asked.

"I'm sure it's not," Ashin said, but he wasn't.

Mateo picked up a stone about the size of a baseball, and threw it with two hands into the fence. There were no sparks, as one might see in a movie, but there was a reaction. Before the rock had fallen to the ground, a siren blared, and searchlights came on, illuminating twenty feet of sidewalk.

Ashin heard a window open, and a voice called from the house, "Get away from there! I'm calling the police!"

He couldn't locate from which window the voice had come, but Ashin called back, "Sorry!" and he nudged Mateo to continue walking.

"Is it safe to keep walking?" Mateo asked.

"Will you throw any more rocks?" Ashin asked.

Mateo didn't answer, but took the lead. Street after street, the fences had been enhanced; they were taller, scarier, and covered with the signs. One sign was even personalized, reading, "We tried, but you kept walking across our lawn, you yelled at our home, and left your trash. We had every right to buy this house."

When they arrived at the park, the found it encircled by a shorter fence, perhaps only five feet tall, with a locked gate. A sign read, "Park open from 9 A.M. to sunset" and "No dogs, no picnics, no sports" and "No beach access."

Ashin dropped his head. He felt such sadness. The town and its people had gone mad. All his life, this community had been smiles, happy waves, small talk with neighbors and shop owners. In the past, even the mistakes had been made in an effort at improving the community. This toxic individualism, this pride of possession overtaking pride in community, this cult of paranoia and posture of manic-defense, this politics-as-plaything and courtroom-as-cudgel, was destroying everything Paris had represented for generations. Perhaps what bothered Ashin the most was that he himself felt a need to go home and hole-up in his house.

"What do we do?" Mateo asked.

Ashin said, "I simply don't know."

They turned for home.

22

Ashin and Mateo were sitting on the front steps. Even the fences running through their immediate neighborhood had grown in height and formidability. There were still no fences in front of Ashin's place, nor at the Funk house.

"Your mother isn't going to put one up?" Ashin asked.

"She says she doesn't see the point. She says, 'If every other rat is in a cage, the last rat is in a cage, too,'" Mateo said.

"Can I ask how your father is doing?" Ashin asked.

"I don't know. I haven't heard from him. Mom talks to him on the phone, but really low, with a serious voice. She won't talk about him," Mateo said, "She just focuses on her work."

There was suddenly shouting and screaming coming from the Glerter property.

"Let's go see," Mateo said, and he headed that way.

"Wait," was all Ashin had time to say, and then he followed the boy.

As Ashin and Mateo arrived at the Glerter's fence, he saw the Glerters as they appeared from around their house, still within their own tall fences. They were half-dressed, both of them were topless, and they were walking quickly with arms outstretched in front of them. They hurriedly began hosing each other off. Percy was spraying his wife's face and breasts with the cold hose water, with Violet saying only, "It's helping, don't stop."

"Mateo, come away from there," Ashin said.

Mateo didn't even look away.

"Oh my God," Violet said, covering herself.

Percy said, "We were attacked!"

Ashin asked, "Bees?" He had no idea what might have happened.

"They sprayed us!" Violet said.

"Who did?" Mateo asked.

"Those two idiots! The beach fascists, Silvio and Lopez!" Percy said.

"Pepper spray?" Mateo asked.

"Why did they do that?" Ashin asked.

"We went down to the beach, and those two were patrolling on 4-wheelers! There's barely enough room on the beach to turn around, but there they were, crossing back and forth, challenging people!" Percy said.

Bent over and blinking, holding a beach towel over her breasts, Violet said, "We told them we have every right to be on that beach!"

"They had batons! And bear spray! They told us we were from away, and to get off the beach, or else they'd make us get off! I told them we wouldn't, and they sprayed us!" Percy said.

"That's assault! We're calling the police! The state police, not the Paris police! This place is crazy!" Violet said, and she headed for the house.

Percy followed and said to Violet, "I told you. I told you we should buy the house but not live here. Small town people are nuts."

"Not now, Percy! I can't even see," she said, and they disappeared into the house.

Ashin and Mateo looked at each other. Ashin said, "Let's go. The police will arrive soon. Let's just get out of the way."

They began walking back to the house, and Ashin said, "There is no talking things over anymore. You can't discuss anything with people who are this far gone."

Mateo said, "I know what you mean."

Ashin thought the boy was really talking about his experience with his father, felt sorry for him, and struggled for the right, comforting thing to say to the boy, when Mateo suddenly asked, "She has really big boobs, huh?"

"Mateo! She was in pain and embarrassed. Show some class," Ashin said.

"Sorry," Mateo said, but then looked back at the Glerter house again.

"Having class is a rare thing these days, and it makes everyone feel a little better," Mateo said.

"Aren't rich people classy? They don't always feel good, and they don't make others feel good," Ashin said.

"Rich people don't automatically have it, you can't buy it, and some of the classiest people I've known were on hard times. That's when it really shows, in fact," Ashin said as they reached the front steps, and climbed to the porch. "But there are some people in Paris who are quite wealthy, and are quite classy. Take people one at a time."

"And it doesn't matter how much class others have. Worry about yourself," Ashin said.

"Okay," Mateo said, "But I'm not sure having class gets things done. Being classy doesn't fix things. Seems like it's just a way of being seen by others."

"Class isn't a face you put on. It guides your decision making, even if no one is watching," Ashin said.

Mateo didn't say anything, he just seemed to be contemplating this.

"Want some lemonade to drink while we watch the police arrive?" Ashin asked.

"Sure," Mateo said.

* * *

It was when they began their second glasses of lemonade that a cruiser marked, "Monterey County Sheriff" arrived at the Glerter place.

"It's not California State Police?" Mateo asked.

"CSP don't really exist anymore; they merged with California Highway Patrol. Remember the show CHiPs?" Ashin asked.

Mateo blinked back at him.

Ashin asked, "What year were you born again?"

Mateo said, "Two-thousand…"

"Stop, never mind," Ashin said.

Just then a van drove up, with "KBSV NewsCenter 12" painted on the side.

"TV news?" Mateo asked.

"Oh no," Ashin put his head in his hands.

"What's wrong?" Mateo asked.

"When people hear about the beach fascists, the fences, and so on, gawkers are going to come from far and wide to see the sideshow," Ashin said, "Some will come just to challenge those two idiots on the beach, assuming they're not locked up."

"You think those men will go to jail?"

"Well, if it were just a matter of following the law, I can't see how they could avoid it, but you never know around here. Some pretty serious matters seem to just fade away sometimes," Ashin said.

Mateo looked back out at the news van, and then down the street. "Why would people come to see the fences?" Mateo asked.

"When someone does something different, other people want to look at them. When a group of people start acting strangely, it's even more interesting. When a community goes nuts," Ashin said, pointing at the Glerters and then sweeping a hand at all the fences, "people can't help but to rush in to take a look, and then run home and share what they saw."

"People find 'crazy' interesting, don't they?" Mateo asked.

"It's fear," Ashin said.

"What are they scared of?" Mateo asked.

"At first, people want to know if the crazy people are a threat to them. Crazy people are unpredictable, and human beings like patterns and predictability, just like your mother does. It's one of the main reasons we have science… to find and document predictable patterns, so that we can feel better," Ashin said.

"Do you like science?" Mateo asked.

"I love it. I always have," Ashin said.

"But I thought science was about discovering new stuff. Not about comforting us," Mateo said.

"We say we're trying to understand our world and our universe, but we tend to settle on the most comforting and most convenient conclusions, and we say that the discoveries are firm science. We even call some of them 'laws' until they aren't anymore," Ashin said. "What we can't explain is scary, so we chalk those things up to monsters, witchcraft, gods, space aliens, and conspiracies."

"Seems like there are more and more conspiracy theories," Mateo said.

"Because we're more and more afraid, and as a population we're less and less capable of understanding the latest science. Conspiracies are easier to understand than science, and we get laughed at less today, than people did in the past, for believing in the conspiracies," Ashin said.

"What do you mean?" Mateo said.

"I mean, take fluoride for example. I'm a dentist. When I was your age, Mateo, almost everyone I knew who was older than forty years old didn't have any teeth left. It was a normal part of life, that a person would have dentures before age forty-five. They added fluoride to toothpaste and to the water, and when I retired, I had elderly patients with all their teeth," Ashin said.

"So?" Mateo asked.

"I knew a man once who said I was part of a conspiracy, that the American Dental Association was as well, that fluoride was actually part of a massive plan to turn everyone into passive zombies who wouldn't resist government oppression," Ashin said.

"That's not true, right?" Mateo asked.

"Just the fact that you'd ask that shows how bad the problem is. Fluoride saves teeth. That's the only reason it's in toothpaste and municipal water," Ashin said.

"Why do people say the government wants to control us? I mean, once the government would have total control over everyone, what do they think the government will then force us to do?" Mateo asked.

"They don't have an answer to that. I've asked before, 'Government wants to control us so that we can do what?' and the answer is always something like, 'Whatever they want!' So, the nuts don't know. Like I said, it's about fear, but they can't explain what they're afraid of," Ashin said.

"Did we used to be smarter?" Mateo asked.

"We can learn just as well as we ever could. It began to change when we insisted that whatever we learn be entertaining at the same time. We refused to put in the work to learn the somewhat dry but important stuff. Next, interesting wasn't good enough. It wasn't enough of a high anymore. It had to be titillating, then it had to be scandalous, and then we got to where it had to be enraging to be engaging," Ashin said.

"How can that be fixed?" Mateo asked.

"I'm not sure it can be. Sometimes things can't be fixed, I'm afraid," Ashin said.

A local patrol car from Paris Police Department pulled up then. The reporter and crew descended upon the police officer as he exited his cruiser. He didn't stop for an interview, and instead made his way through the gate, and up to the front door, before entering. The press stayed outside the fence, but the camera operator began shooting footage of the Glerter's fence, the signs, and then the fence at the neighbor's house, and the next house as well.

"Okay, but people scared of fluoride and needing rage to pay attention doesn't explain why people want to come look at crazy people," Mateo said.

"How many times have you heard someone say, 'I'm not crazy, I know what I know!' People are not only worried that crazy people will hurt them, they're also scared that others will think they're crazy. But most of all, people are frightened of actually going insane themselves. We all start off closer or farther from that edge of sanity, we don't quite know where it is, and we're terrified of going over it," Ashin said.

Another Monterey County Sheriff cruiser pulled up, and the deputy went inside.

"The more cops and media show up, the more likely someone is getting arrested," Ashin said.

Less than five minutes later, the local Paris police officer came out, went to his cruiser, and sped away.

"There he goes," Ashin said.

"Where?" Mateo asked.

"To find those two boneheads," Ashin said.

Mateo moved down to the porch floor, laying back on his elbows. He asked, "Why did the beach become so important to them? They've lived here a long time. Why did they go so nuts about the beach?"

Ashin put his lemonade down and said, "I'm not sure. Part of it is probably because of the people moving in, and posting those signs that basically shout, 'This is mine!' and that causes others to protect what they think is theirs. Then there are locals who are taking away space and activities from other locals," Ashin said.

"It's weird," Mateo said.

"What is?" Ashin asked.

"The amount of space didn't shrink, the number of people didn't really grow… but all of a sudden there isn't enough room for everybody," Mateo said.

"Everything, Mateo, is about fear of loss. Loss of land, loss of access, loss of money, loss of love, loss of status, loss of sanity," Ashin said, and then sighed. "Even the loss of time."

23

Just as he sat down in front of his television set, ready for the 6 p.m. start of the Town Council meeting, there was a knock at the door. Ashin went over, opened it, and found Mrs. Kirschner there.

"Mr. Asilomar, I'm sorry to knock on your door so late," she said.

"Not at all, Mrs. Kirschner, what can I do for you? You haven't come to clean?" Ashin said.

"I'm afraid not. In fact, I've come to let you know I won't be able to come by any more. You see, I sold my house a few days ago. I simply couldn't turn the offer down, you know. The money is already in my bank account. Quite remarkable really, but the problem is even with all that money, there isn't another house in the area that I can afford," she said.

"I see," he said, remembering what Mitch had said.

"So, I'm afraid I'll be moving. To Missouri, to live with my sister," she said.

Ashin said, "Oh, well, that will be lovely, I'm sure."

"I'm so sorry about the short notice, but I'm in a hotel room now. All my belongings are in storage. I've got to do something," she said.

"Of course," Ashin said.

"And my sister tells me my money will go far in Waynesville," she said.

"I've never heard of it," Ashin said.

"It's in the Ozarks, so that should be nice," she said.

"Ah yes," Ashin said.

There was a pause, and then she said, "Well, I'll be going. Thank you for everything, and again, sorry about the short notice."

"That's quite alright," Ashin said.

"Oh, and you can keep any of my Tupperware that you might still have," she said, and turned away, waving over her shoulder. "Bye now, take care."

"You, too, Mrs. Kirschner," Ashin said. He watched her walk down the steps, and then to the road, where she climbed into her car, and was off. He stood there for a moment, looking down the road, and then scanning all the fences. He looked over at the Funk house, wondering where Mateo was, and then he withdrew inside.

Ashin returned to his chair, just as the developer, Cyrus Eliason, began to speak.

"I have considered the council's feedback, and we've modified the design of our proposal. We have added additional two-bedroom apartments to the project," Eliason said.

Several members of the Town Council nodded in agreement, and one asked, "How many of the thirty apartments will have two-bedrooms in the updated design?"

Eliason took a breath, and then said, "Four."

The councilors looked at each other, and then back at Eliason.

Boothby Baxter asked, "How many?"

"Four," Eliason said again.

"Mr. Eliason," said a council member, "we thought that you might take our concerns seriously."

Ashin turned off the television. He thought either they would compromise, or they wouldn't, but it wouldn't happen on live local TV this evening. It would likely happen in phone calls in the coming weeks, and so-called workshops, not broadcast on television, and scheduled when most people were working and unable to attend. The results would be unveiled in a regular meeting, public input would be heard, maybe a petition would circulate, but Ashin knew that any new housing was a long way off.

24

The next day, Ashin went to get Mateo for a walk. The walks were less pleasant now, like a stroll through a canyon of chain link, but he needed the exercise to control his blood sugar levels, and he thought the exercise would be good for the boy's lungs.

He knocked on the Funk's front door, and June opened it.

"Good morning, Mrs. Funk," Ashin said.

"Please, call me June. With any luck, I won't be Mrs. Funk for very much longer," she said.

"Ah, I'm sorry," Ashin said.

"I'm afraid it's long overdue," she said.

Ashin said, "Again, I'm sorry. I've come to see if Mateo would like to go for a walk."

"It's crazy out there, isn't it? Are you sure it's even safe to walk anymore? Violet was pepper-sprayed on the beach. The two men were arrested, but they're out on bail now," she said.

"We won't go near the beach. Just a stroll on the

sidewalks," Ashin said, "But if you feel he shouldn't come along, I certainly understand."

"I do worry, but I think Mateo getting out of the house and getting some air is a good thing," she said, and then she called for Mateo.

"At the first sign of trouble, we'll head straight back," Ashin said.

"Oh good, please do," she said.

After a momentary silence, June asked, "Did you see the Town Council meeting last night?"

"Yes, the four two-bedroom apartments," Ashin said.

"That too! But I meant the leather shop, what they did to that poor woman. All she wants to do is open a business in this town," June said.

"I didn't see that part. What happened?" Ashin asked.

"Well, Shelley came to them with a bunch of plans and paperwork, including sources of her leather," June said.

"Right," Ashin said.

"Remember, that was an issue with the council? They wanted to know where the leather was coming from?" June asked.

Ashin said, "I remember, yes."

"So, she reported that the sources of her leather are both Canadian and Italian," June said, and then fell silent.

Ashin waited a moment, and asked, "And?"

June said, "So, one of the council members immediately asked, 'No domestic leather? Don't you love America?'"

"For Heaven's sake," Ashin said, rubbing his eyes.

"Then another councilor said, 'I can't believe we're still talking about real animal skins. It's barbaric. How would any of us like it if someone was wearing our skin around town? Can't we ever put Mother Nature first?'" June said.

Mateo then appeared.

June said, "Can you imagine? No wonder I work from home."

"There certainly seem to be unnecessary hurdles for someone wanting to launch a new business in Paris," Ashin said.

"It sure seems that way," she said, and then there was an awkward pause.

"Let's go," Mateo said.

"You be careful. A lot of loonies out there," June said, and went into the house.

Mateo and Ashin headed off down the street.

25

As they walked, Ashin noticed something different hanging on the twelve-foot-high fences, topped with razor wire. New signs had been added. The first one read only, "Danger!"

"So, *now* they're electrified?" Mateo asked.

"They look like normal chain link fences to me," Ashin said.

Around the corner, they found a white sign that read, "Stay out. Booby traps on premises. You have been warned."

"No way!" Mateo said. "People can build booby traps?"

"It's illegal. You can't set up booby traps, not even on your own property. You can go to prison, and anyone hurt by your traps can bring a lawsuit, and they will almost surely win," Ashin said.

"Even if they were coming to rob you?" Mateo asked.

"Even if they admit in court that they were on your property to rob you, if they got hurt in your booby trap, they will likely win the lawsuit. It's happened before," Ashin said.

The next sign was red and triangular, and it read, "Mines. Minas. Danger. Peligro."

"Like, landmines?" Mateo asked.

"It can't be true," Ashin said, looking through the fence. He could see small earthen mounds scattered around the lawn.

"Seems like a sign that warns about landmines should use exclamation marks, not periods," Mateo said.

"You say the weirdest things," Ashin said. Looking through the fence, he could also see something else.

"What are those?" Mateo asked, pointing.

"Looks like guard dogs," Ashin said.

"There's one near that telephone pole! Outside the fence!" Mateo said.

Ashin squinted, taking a hard look.

"Why are they so still?" Mateo asked.

"They're stuffed. They're toy dogs. Toys, standing ready in a minefield, and on patrol," Ashin said. Maybe three-feet tall, the stuffed animals looked like German Shepherds, two sitting among the mounds, silently watching the fence, while the third seemed to be waiting, partially obscured, to ambush.

"What good does that do?" Mateo asked.

"Maybe just to scare people initially. Or maybe it's a statement they're making to the town about the dog ordinances," Ashin said.

"And you think I'm weird?" Mateo asked.

"Want to keep walking?" Ashin asked.

"It's not as relaxing as it used to be," Mateo said, but then he added, "It's like we're getting ready for war. Maybe my father has the right idea."

"Want to head toward the carousel?" Ashin asked.

Mateo didn't answer, but he started walking, and Ashin followed.

"The whole town has changed. Why don't the police or the Town Council do something about all this?" Mateo asked.

"The changes have come faster than town government can keep up," Ashin said.

"They pass dog rules fast enough. They need a fence rule. Someone has to do something," Mateo said.

Ashin looked up and down the street, with fences as far as the eye could see. "It would certainly cause an uproar now if the town developed a fence ordinance. A lot of money has been spent. Plus, people get addicted."

Mateo asked, "Addicted to what?"

"A sense of security. Once people come to believe they need something to be safe, or even just to add to their safety, it's awful tough to get them to part with it," Ashin said.

"But some of this is stupid. Stuffed guard dogs," Mateo said.

"It doesn't matter how stupid. I bet you it kicks off an arms race to have more stuffed dogs than the neighbor does, or bigger stuffed dogs," Ashin said.

"What's an arms race?" Mateo asked.

"Doesn't matter," Ashin said, "Also, people have to win, even when it's really losing."

"Like what?" Mateo asked.

"There used to be these online auction websites," Ashin said.

"I think there still are," Mateo said.

"So, back when they first started, people could actually find good deals on those. Like an item selling in a store for $50 might be sold online slightly used, and when the bidding was over, it would go for $40," Ashin said.

"Sounds good," Mateo said.

"Well, nowadays, that item you can get in the store for $50 will sell in an online auction for $70," Ashin said.

"Why pay more for it online?" Mateo asked.

"Because it's about winning now, and not about saving money. People aren't looking for a bargain. They bid $50 for an item worth $50, and when another person's bid comes in for $60, they get competitive and bid $65. We can't self-moderate anymore. We take being outbid as someone trampling on us, looking down on us, taking from us. We up our bid as if to prove we won't take abuse from anyone, but instead we're just acting like spoiled children," Ashin said.

Mateo didn't say anything for a minute or two, and then asked, "Okay, again, how do we fix all this?"

"Like I said, I'm not sure it can be fixed," Ashin said. "The system may need to get burned down and rebuilt from scratch."

"Huh?" Mateo asked.

"Just an expression," Ashin said, remembering the story about the Funk garage in Texas.

They came to the carousel, and went inside. The wooden horses were still, and the platform dark. They walked past the windows of the candy makers, with no activity inside any of the shops, and where the record store had been, there was simply an empty space behind the glass. Even the booth was missing.

"Where'd it all go?" Mateo said.

"The candy shops look closed, but this one is definitely shut down. I guess he couldn't make enough to keep things going," Ashin said.

Mateo looked up and asked again, "What's an arm's race?"

"It's when two countries are competing to have the most weapons, or the best weapons," Ashin said.

"So, the minefields," Mateo said.

"Right."

"Yeah, but, what comes after mines?" Mateo asked.

Ashin had no idea. "Let's head back."

"How does a country win an arms race?" Mateo asked.

"When the other country gives up, and can't afford to keep going," Ashin said.

"So, it's not really a battle with weapons. It's more like a battle of money to build or buy weapons, but not use them," Mateo said.

"I suppose so."

Mateo paused, and then said, "What a waste. It would be better to start over, like you said."

Ashin said, "Sometimes a fresh start is better than a repair job."

"Yeah, I always thought the saying, 'It's as good as new' was a lie. Nothing is ever as good as new," Mateo said.

"Sometimes things are better if you break them in a bit though," Ashin said.

As they began the walk home, they both looked up the street lined with fences, and Ashin said, "But this, I'm afraid, is simply broken."

26

The next day, Ashin was putting away his dishes when there was a knock at the door. It was Mitch Mitchell.

"Hey Mitch, what can I do for you?" Ashin asked, inviting the man in.

"There are almost no houses left to sell," Mitch said.

"At least the Funk house next door didn't put up those fences. That's three of us," Ashin said. Mitch suddenly looked sheepish.

"You didn't," Ashin said.

"It seemed to be the thing to do. I got to thinking if someone wanted to do harm, I didn't want to be the only house in my neighborhood that looked unprotected," Mitch said.

Ashin shook his head, staring at the floor. He said, "Well, I guess you could try selling them all again. I bet the Glerter couple would be interested in selling."

"I heard about that. Called them up. They've already moved out, but they're not interested in selling. They figure they'll just let it sit awhile. Those types of folks, they have a philosophy of 'never sell land.' They say the grandchildren's grandchildren will thank them," Mitch said.

"Oh, they have children?" Ashin asked.

"No," Mitch said, and then fell silent.

"So, what's next? Are you going to sell your house?" Ashin asked.

"We're taking offers until tomorrow afternoon," Mitch said.

"Are they high?" Ashin asked.

Mitch said, "Won't officially know until then, but people have been calling me, making verbal offers. Some are more than fifty percent over asking price. One guy said his wife is pregnant, and in addition to a huge offer, he said they'd be willing to sign a contract promising to name the kid 'Mitch Mitchell,' and their last name isn't even Mitchell!"

"What if it's a girl?" Ashin asked.

"The guy said it wouldn't matter," Mitch said.

"Will you accept?" Ashin asked.

"That's creepy, Doc," Mitch said.

"I agree. Where will you go after you sell?" Ashin asked.

"I'm going to retire. Somewhere quiet. I'm looking for a small cabin on a lake somewhere. Until I find it, I'll move in with my brother and his wife. After all this, I need a change," Mitch said, "Are you really going to stay?"

"I am sad that the town is so different now. It's not how I pictured living out my days, looking at these fences, with people hiding indoors," Ashin said.

"That won't last that long. The fences are a fad. Once they start coming down, no one will want to be the last one with a prison fence out front," Mitch said, "Two years, tops."

"Carousel was closed yesterday, and all the shops," Ashin said.

"The folks that ran all those places sold their houses and moved. The people that bought the houses all work on their computers inside their newly fenced-in homes. The Hart family is still hoping someone will buy, or even rent, the carousel itself. Maybe the town will pick it up as an indoor park," Mitch said.

"The town will never keep it up like the family did," Ashin said.

"It's true, and someday the carousel will be nothing more than memories, part of the saga of the Hart family," Mitch said, and then gesturing toward the Funk house, he asked, "How about your little friend?"

"The father moved out, and got his own apartment," Ashin said.

"I heard he's already being evicted from that apartment. He told the new owners that money isn't real anyway, that we all die in debt, that the Earth doesn't belong to people, and that everyone has a right to a home, and if he has a right to something, it doesn't make sense he has to pay for it," Mitch said.

Ashin looked over toward the house, and imagined Mateo inside. "Really? I hadn't heard," he said. "Do you know how long until he has to go?"

"They served him with a three-day yesterday, but the owners didn't go through the correct process. That'd take over a month, you know? I think they either didn't know, being from away and all, or they're hoping he doesn't know and that he'll just leave," Mitch said.

"And come back here," Ashin said.

"You live right next door, and you didn't hear?" Mitch asked.

"I hadn't," Ashin said, "Where'd you hear it?"

"From Almira Benton… you'll be happy to know she's not selling either, you get to keep her," Mitch said.

"Terrific," Ashin said.

"Anyway, she told me that Funk came by, and the wife chased him off," Mitch said.

"When was this?"

"Yesterday," Mitch said.

Ashin thought it must have happened while he and Mateo were down at the carousel, and he was glad for it.

"She followed him right across the front lawn, big old cleaver in her hand, raised above her head!" Mitch said.

"Oh no," Ashin said, "What a mess."

"Have you seen the kid since yesterday? Maybe they hightailed it?" Mitch asked.

Both men looked out the window at the Funk house, and just then Mateo came out. The boy disappeared and reappeared with his bicycle.

"I've never seen him ride it," Ashin said.

"A bit small for him," Mitch said.

"What's he got in the basket?" Ashin said.

"Looks like a big Mason jar of water," Mitch said, and Mateo pedaled off.

"What in the world?" Ashin asked.

It was quiet for a moment, and then Mitch said, "Well,

I won't move away without dropping by once more to give you one last chance to list this place."

Ashin held out his hand, and Mitch took it. "Okay, Mitch, check in, and let me know if you decide to accept that naming-the-baby thing."

"Will do," Mitch said, and then headed out the door.

Ashin looked out the window, not at Mitch, but in the direction that Mateo had gone. He decided he'd go for a walk, and maybe run into the boy. He walked down to the park. The gate was open, and he entered. He went to the off-leash dog pen, but there was no one using it. There were no joggers, no picnickers, no dogs anywhere, and no musicians. He spotted Dorothy Rieger, a retired professor and friend of Rebecca's, sitting alone on a bench. Ashin approached her.

"Morning, Dottie. Certainly quiet these days," he said.

"Good morning. It sure is. I especially miss the young people busking," Dottie said.

"I wondered if anyone was still coming to this place," Ashin said.

"Those young musicians... it's such a hopeful thing, making music for people, perhaps wishing someday to be playing for larger audiences. But they came here, with their instruments, and played because they couldn't imagine not performing," she said.

"I miss the people throwing Frisbees for their dogs. There was so much joy. For the owner, for the dog, and for the people who sat and watched. What acrobats some of those dogs were," Ashin said.

"And people napping in the sun, with the sound of the surf. Peaceful," Dottie said.

Ashin listened and couldn't hear the waves, and he looked out to sea.

"The water is still today," she said.

Ashin said, "It's quiet."

"But not peaceful," she said.

"So, we've still got the physical space, but the park has lost its hopefulness, its joy, and its peace," Ashin said.

Dottie smiled sadly, and said, "Maybe we'll come to our senses, and they will all return."

"Maybe the town could organize an event, perhaps even a concert," Ashin said.

"Wouldn't be the same. That's like watching deer in a meadow versus cows in a field. The nature of the gathering is different. I'm afraid I prefer the organic," Dottie said.

Ashin paused, and then asked, "Have you seen a boy come by, on a bicycle?"

A pair of pigeons landed nearby, and Dottie watched them. "Aside from you, Ashin, those pigeons are the only other living souls I've seen down here."

He nodded, and said, "Have a nice day, Dottie. We'll see you," and turned to walk away.

"You most likely won't. Take care, Ashin," she said, still watching the pigeons.

Ashin began to say something, but didn't, and instead he headed to the sidewalk.

27

The Town Council met that Wednesday, and Ashin decided to attend in person. He didn't get on the official agenda, but he thought he'd ask a question during the "public comments" portion of the meeting. Unfortunately, that came at the end. Ashin was sure they did that in the hopes that many of those who attended, intending to speak, would get bored and leave before they had the opportunity.

He sat in one of the six folding chairs, and not at the table. There was only one other person present. It was Almira Benton.

The chair gaveled the meeting into session. Members of the council were missing, and even Boothby Baxter was not present.

"Having the minimum number of councilors present for a quorum, we can proceed, but Charlie called and said he wanted to be present for the first three agenda items, and so he asked if we could take those up at a later meeting," the chair said.

"So moved," said one.

"Second," said another.

"All in favor?" the chair asked, and all the hands went up.

"That leaves us with the one agenda item Charlie didn't care about, yet another issue with dogs. Mrs. Benton, what is it this time?" the chair said.

"You needn't take that tone," Almira Benton said, standing, "There is a matter concerning these stuffed guard dogs."

"You can't be serious," the chair said.

"Quite serious. It's a safety issue," she said.

"What isn't a safety issue?" Ashin said.

"It's my turn to talk," she said, glaring at Ashin.

The chair sounded bored and exasperated, but said, "Doc, you can have your say, but you'll have to wait until she's done."

"Sorry. I don't have anything to say about the dangerous stuffed toy guard dogs, it just slipped out," Ashin said.

The council members chuckled, but Almira Benton was not amused. She said, "This is not a laughing matter. Michael Haven was startled by one of those dogs, hiding behind a mailbox on the sidewalk, and crashed his bicycle into a parked car. He broke his thumb."

"Mrs. Benton, Mike was half in the bag when that happened. You know he drinks. He's more upset about the two broken bottles of whiskey he was carrying than his thumb. Why do you think he has to take a bike to market?" the chair asked.

"That's beside the point," she said, her voice rising,

"That could have been a child on a bicycle, startled into traffic, and now that I've brought it to your attention, and it's in the public record, if you don't act... God forbid a child is hurt and you didn't act this evening when you had the chance."

She dramatically took her seat. *One of the most powerful forces in America,* Ashin thought, *is fear of liability. She's going to win this.*

The chair looked at Ashin, and asked, "Anything to add, Doc?"

"By all means, Mr. Chairman, save us from these wayward stuffed animals," Ashin said.

The chair looked around, and one councilor said, "I move that the town ordinance regarding dogs be amended to add that any stuffed guard dog..."

Almira Benton stood again and said, "Even a life-size cardboard cutout might have the same dangerous effect."

The councilor paused, and then said, "That any representation of a dog, in any form, must be contained within one's own property."

Almira Benton stood again, and Ashin couldn't help himself, "For Heaven's sake, sit down, Almira."

"Don't you talk to me that way!" she said.

"Mrs. Benton, sit down. We've heard enough. There's a motion on the floor already. You can't edit the motion in real time. I suggest you simply run for council next go around. You make it to more meetings than some of us anyway," the chair said.

She looked like she might say something, but didn't, and she sat.

The chair asked, “Do I hear a second?”

“Second,” said another councilor.

“All in favor?”

Hands went up.

“The motion passes, the ordinance is thus amended. That takes us to public comments. Mrs. Benton, have you anything else to say?” the chair asked.

She only shook her head, but she didn’t leave.

“Doc?” the chair asked.

Ashin slowly stood and said, “I only wanted to say that while you’re passing ordinances, you might consider passing a few more, so that we might begin to restore Paris to what it once was.”

“Such as?” the chair asked.

“Perhaps an ordinance on fence height. Or one against the use of razor wire. Maybe something that doesn’t allow signs to threaten passersby,” Ashin said.

“Free speech,” Almira Benton said.

Ashin ignored her. “How about an ordinance that ensures public access to public spaces, like the beaches?”

“Property rights,” Almira Benton said.

“His turn to speak, Mrs. Benton,” the chair said.

“How about in certain zones, a requirement that a home be occupied for at least six months of the year? Or a ban on short-term rentals unless the owner lives on the premises?” Ashin asked. One councilman appeared upset by this.

“How about checking to see if property owners are voting in Paris, and also in the town or city where they spend most of their year?” Ashin asked.

“They have to prove residency,” a council member said.

"They can do that with a fishing license," Ashin said. "What if you checked where they pay income tax?"

"Why not just leave well enough alone?" a council member asked.

"Like leashing the stuffed animals? While the town converted itself into what looks like an armed camp, you did nothing. The joy we used to see in the park with families… and their dogs… picnicking and having fun is gone because you let one old crank threaten you with lawsuits," Ashin said.

"They're expensive to defend, even when they are ridiculous," the chair said.

"They are not ridiculous," Almira Benton said.

"Of course they are," the chair said.

"But you let her cower you with them. Sometimes it's expensive to fight back, but the first time you caved, you only encouraged her to keep coming in here with the next issue, and the next issue. Every time you have backed down to her, and people like her, the entire community has lost something, and she was encouraged further," Ashin said. "Stand up for the town, for God's sake. Fight back."

"Well, I never," Almira Benton said.

"I move we strike the new amendment to the dog ordinance we just approved," a council member said.

"Second," said another.

"All in favor?" the chair asked, and all the hands went up.

"How dare you?" Almira Benton asked Ashin.

"Great, stuffed animals are now allowed to roam free again. But at least you've lost one, Almira," Ashin said.

“I am going to court with this,” she said.

“To have stuffed dogs restrained? Please do begin with that one, so the court knows who they’re dealing with,” Ashin said.

“I’ll sue you as well,” she said.

“For what?” Ashin asked.

“Slander! You called me a ‘crank,’” she said.

“I can call you something much worse, if you like,” Ashin said.

“This is all on television,” Almira Benton said, standing, “You’ll all be sorry.” She turned and walked out.

“That was a bit out of line, don’t you think, Doc?” the chair asked.

“Thank you for freeing the toys, gentlemen. Why don’t you consider some of the other things you might do?” Ashin asked as he rose. “Try to help Paris be a community again. I’m not sure it can be fixed, but at least try.”

28

When Ashin came out onto his front porch to see what all the fuss was about, he spotted Mateo already crossing the lawn. Just then, a second cruiser from the Paris Police Department came racing by, with siren blaring and lights flashing, and then it turned down towards the beach.

"Mateo!" Ashin called.

Mateo stopped, looked back, and waited. Ashin caught up with the boy, and they both headed the way the police car had gone.

"What do you think is going on?" Mateo asked. "Aren't those two guys from the beach in jail?"

"They got out on bail, while they wait for their court dates. I'm sure those two are playing it very cool, though. They wouldn't want to make things worse for themselves. This must be something else," Ashin said, but as they arrived at the beach, he realized he was wrong. Chuy Lopez was operating a loader, and David Silvio was on the ground guiding him. It was extreme low tide, and the men had nearly completed placing a new seawall of large concrete blocks at the water's edge.

Ashin and Mateo cautiously approached as one police officer was talking to Silvio, while the other was motioning for Lopez to stop.

"This is our beach! If every part of the beach that's covered at high tide has to be shared with the public, okay, but we're lowering that line so we can take back our beach!" Silvio said.

The cop he was shouting to, over the sound of the loader, said, "Davy, that's really dumb! You realize when you're done that your beach won't have access to the water? You're turning it into a sandbox!"

"At least it'll be *our* private sandbox!" Silvio said, "Put it here!" Silvio pointed, and Lopez dropped the enormous block. With perhaps three more, the beach would be cut off from the ocean, from one cliff to the other. Ashin and Mateo stopped and watched.

Lopez turned the loader around to retrieve the next block. While one cop stayed to discuss the situation with Silvio, the other, who had been trying to get Lopez's attention, sprinted alongside the large, yellow equipment as it drove across the sand. A third police officer arrived, and seeing where the Lopez was headed, drove his cruiser into the loader's path. It came to a stop, but then it suddenly lurched forward. Lopez attempted to drive across the hood of the police car, but instead of going up and over it, the huge tires were pushing the cruiser sideways. The occupant police officer, jumping clear of his car, drew his weapon, as did the police officer who had been following alongside. They both opened fire on the cab, and more than ten shots rang out between the two of them.

Ashin dropped to the sand, and reached to pull Mateo down with him, but was too late. Mateo's head whipped back, he cried out, and the boy fell. The loader stopped, the engine rumbling low.

"Mateo!" Ashin said, lunging over to the boy.

"Oh my God!" one of the police officers said, running toward them, already calling for an ambulance on his radio.

Ashin slowly rolled Mateo onto his back, and there was blood on the sand.

"Easy!" the cop said.

Silvio and the other cop arrived at a run, sliding to a stop in the sand on their knees.

Mateo quickly sat up.

"Whoa, whoa," the officer said.

Mateo had a cut across his right cheek, bleeding profusely, but was clearly only grazed. He looked at the nearest police officer and asked, "You shot me?"

The officer, pulling on his gloves, and then pressing a bandage against Mateo's cheek, said, "Must have ricocheted. Are you hurt anywhere else?"

Mateo looked down, while Silvio and the other police officer scanned Mateo's back and arms.

"I don't think so," Mateo said.

"There's an ambulance on the way," the officer said.

Ashin looked Mateo in the eyes, and the boy said, "My dad is right. We do need a bunker."

The door to the cab on the loader opened.

"Is the guy in there dead?" Mateo asked.

Ashin looked back and saw Lopez's hands held high to the roof of the loader's cab. The nearest police officer pulled him down, and onto his belly on the beach.

"He's not dead," Ashin said.

"I'm the only one who got shot?" Mateo asked.

"Just a ricochet. No one was shooting at you," the officer said.

There was a clicking, and Ashin looked up to see that Silvio was being put in handcuffs as well.

"Why is he being arrested?" Mateo asked.

"They'll think of something," Ashin said.

The ambulance arrived, and two EMTs sprinted to Ashin, Mateo, and the others.

One EMT asked, "What have we got?"

Mateo said, "The police shot me in the face, but I'm okay."

"Ricochet," the officer said again.

"Anyone else hurt?" the second EMT asked.

"They only shot me," Mateo said, and the policeman sighed.

The EMT took a look at the wound, put a new bandage on it, and said, "You'll need a few stitches. Are you Grandpa?"

Ashin shook his head, and said, "I'll let his mother know. You're going to Peninsula Hospital?"

"Yep," the EMT said, "Can you walk?"

Mateo said, "I think they only shot me in my face."

The EMT stood, holding the bandage to Mateo's cheek while others helped Mateo to his feet. "If you feel lightheaded or anything, just let me know, okay?"

Mateo nodded.

Lopez was already seated in an undamaged cruiser. He said, "This is a war! Don't you understand? We are trying to save everything, before the outsiders destroy it all!"

Silvio said, "Shut up, Chuy! The kid got hurt!"

"Jesus, the cops shot the kid?" Lopez asked.

The police officer said only, "Dammit."

Lopez said, "You're supposed to 'serve and protect' but you haven't done anything, except hurt a kid, and you haven't stopped these people from away! They're trying to erase Paris!"

"I think maybe it needs to be," Mateo said.

"This is way out of hand," Ashin said.

Once Silvio was also in a cruiser, and Mateo had climbed up into the ambulance, the boy called back, "You're coming to the hospital, right?"

"I'll go tell your mother, and then I'll head over," Ashin said.

"Ooh man, that's going to be intense. Get ready," Mateo said, the ambulance door closed, and it pulled away.

A police officer, the one who had handcuffed Lopez, asked Ashin, "Could I get your names, please?"

"I'm Ashin Asilomar, the boy is Mateo Funk," Ashin said.

"Funk? Related to Deepak Funk?" the officer asked.

"Why? What's happened?" Ashin asked.

"He calls 911 every day with some new crazy thing to report," the officer said.

"That'd be him," Ashin said.

"Do you live in Paris?" he asked, writing in a notepad.

"The Funks and I are neighbors here," Ashin said, "I live at 2905 David Avenue."

"Phone number," the cop asked, and Ashin told him.

"Thank you. I'm sure a detective will be in touch," the officer said.

Ashin watched as the police officer turned and walked past the damaged cruiser. He climbed into a different car, and it drove away.

Ashin looked back. Everyone was gone. Silvio and Lopez hadn't closed off the entire beach from the ocean, so the tide would still get in. He looked over at the twelve-foot gap on one end of the new seawall. *It will fill differently now, and empty differently, too. Even failing, they changed the whole thing,* he thought.

Ashin walked back up to the street, and to the Funk house. He knocked on the door, and June Funk answered.

Looking past Ashin, she asked, "Oh no! Where is Mateo?"

"He's been hurt, but not badly. He's got a cut on his face, but it doesn't appear serious. He's in an ambulance on his way to Peninsula Hospital right now," Ashin said.

June shrieked, and asked, "If it's not bad, why an ambulance?"

"I probably could have brought him home, and you could have driven him, but the police officer called an ambulance, just to be safe," Ashin said.

"Police officer! What happened?" June asked.

"Why don't we head over to the hospital, and I'll tell you one the way?" Ashin asked.

"Okay, okay, I need my bag!" she said.

"And shoes," Ashin said.

"Of course, and keys!"

Ashin said, "I'll drive."

"Okay, okay," she said.

Once June Funk had her bag, and was wearing shoes, they were underway. Driving, Ashin said, "Two men were down at the beach causing a problem."

"Was it those two men who sprayed the Glerters?" she asked.

"Same guys. The police responded," Ashin said.

"Okay, yeah, I heard the sirens," she said.

"So did Mateo. I saw him heading across the grass, on his way to the beach to investigate, so I went with him," Ashin said, "When we got down there, the police were trying to deal with those two, when one of them rammed a police cruiser with a large piece of equipment. In response, the police fired on that equipment."

"Oh my God! My Mateo has been shot!" she said.

"Apparently, there was a ricochet that grazed his cheek. The police began caring for him immediately, and called for an ambulance, which got there quickly. The EMT thinks that Mateo needs a few stitches," Ashin said.

"So, he doesn't have a bullet in him! Right? Grazed means it barely touched him, right?" she asked.

"That's right. It might not have even been an entire bullet. Or it might have even been a piece of glass or something from the loader," Ashin said.

"Okay, good, okay good. But it came so close to him!" she said, as they pulled into the Emergency Room parking lot. He let her out right by the door, and went to park. She sprinted inside, forgetting her bag in the car, so Ashin carried it in. He found her at the reception desk.

"So, can I be with him?" she asked.

"Please fill these out first. Do you have insurance?" the woman behind the counter asked.

"Okay," June said, and began quickly filling out the form, and then said, "My card, it's in my bag."

Ashin handed it over.

"Good, good, thank you," June said, and finished filling out the paperwork.

"Alright, he's just down the hall, I'll take you," the woman said, and then looked at Ashin and asked, "Family?"

June immediately said, "Yes."

The three of them walked passed closed doors, and Ashin could hear muffled voices, and one unseen patient cried out.

Then, Ashin heard Mateo's voice. He was singing, "She wants pretty horses, gets monkeys instead. She's a poet in a circus, who's trapped in her head."

June said, "That song he keeps singing."

Ashin said, "From the lady in Texas."

"What lady?" June asked.

Ashin was about to relay what Mateo had told him, but the woman knocked on the exam room door, opened it, and said, "Mateo, your family is here." She stepped aside, and let June and Ashin in, and closed the door behind them as she left.

Two women in scrubs were caring for Mateo. The wound had pretty much stopped bleeding, and it was cleaned up.

"Are you Mom?" one asked, and then said, "I'm Dr. McQuarrie. He's going to be fine. He was just singing to us. He does need some stitches, but other than that, he's okay."

"Thank you so much. Thank you. I'm June. He has cystic fibrosis," June said, and then stepped to Mateo, gripped his hand, and kissed his forehead, careful to keep her hair away from his wound.

Mateo said, "Hi, Mom."

"He told us. It'll be just local anesthetic, we don't need to put him under or anything. Right across the hall, there's a little room with comfortable chairs, coffee, water. Please help yourselves, and I'll come and get you when we're done," Dr. McQuarrie said.

"Will there be a big scar?" June asked.

"Mom," Mateo said.

"Would you prefer we consult with a plastic surgeon? She might even be in the building," Dr. McQuarrie said.

The other woman in scrubs said, "Oh, I don't think so, I think she's at her office today."

"Still, that's only three miles from here. Would you prefer I give her a call, and check her availability?" Dr. McQuarrie asked.

"I don't want that," Mateo said. "I want like a legit scar. That'd be cool."

Ashin chuckled. June asked Mateo, "Could we split the difference?" and then to Dr. McQuarrie, "I'm sure you'll do just fine, doctor."

Ashin held the door open, and June headed for it.

"We'll take good care of him. It won't be long," Dr. McQuarrie said.

Ashin and June went into the waiting room, and sat. Ashin asked, "Want something to drink?"

"I could use a stiff drink," June said.

Ashin smiled, but then June asked, "Why didn't you stop him from going down there?"

"How? Tackle him?" Ashin asked.

"Just by telling him not to go," June said.

Ashin leaned in a bit, and gently said, "He was going, no matter what I said. My only choice was to go with him or not, so I went."

June was quiet for a moment, and then said, "I'm sorry. You're right, of course. I've always worried about him, but he has always done what all the other kids do. Except for the coughing, PT, and the enzymes he takes with meals, he's been a pretty normal kid."

Ashin said, "I like that he isn't completely normal." He smiled, and she smiled back.

"When he was just a baby, a newborn really, he just kept throwing up. He was so sick," June said.

"When did you find out what it was?" Ashin said.

"They test now, but back then, they didn't. They thought it was allergies to formula, and all sorts of other guesses. One day, a young doctor was holding him. I was exhausted, and this young man was cradling Mateo in his arms, and then he kissed the baby on the forehead. I thought it was the sweetest thing. But it wasn't," June said.

"What do you mean?" Ashin asked.

"It was salty. Mateo was salty. The young doctor handed the baby back to me, and sort of hurried out, without telling me at the time about the salty kiss," June said.

"People with CF are salty?" Ashin asked.

"It's a big part of what's going on. Salt actually builds up, and prevents them from clearing by coughing, and the mess leads to respiratory infections. The skin of people with CF is often incredibly salty. It even bleaches his clothes sometimes," June said.

"I never knew that," Ashin said.

There was a pause in the conversation, and then Ashin asked, "Are you going to tell his father about this?"

June looked at the floor.

"Want me to tell him?" Ashin asked.

June took a deep breath and said, "Deepak is a sick man. I'm afraid he's had a breakdown. I'm not really speaking with him much."

"Well, just the same, why don't I go down to his apartment, and let him know?" Ashin asked.

June looked him in the eyes and said, "It might not even be safe."

Ashin nodded, and said, "I understand."

Then they sat, mostly silently, until the door opened, with Mateo in his street clothes, and a white bandage on his cheek.

"Does it hurt?" Ashin asked.

"Nope," Mateo said.

Dr. McQuarrie stepped in behind him and said, "It probably will. I'm giving him a prescription for some painkillers, but if he needs them, it'll probably just be overnight. You can manage any pain tomorrow with acetaminophen or ibuprofen. The bandage can come off tomorrow, too, but no showers for a week."

"Man, that's awesome," Mateo said, grinned, and

then brought his hand up to his bandage.

"Only baths, and you have to be very careful not to get the cut and stitches wet," Dr. McQuarrie said.

Mateo looked a bit disappointed.

"If the area starts to look red, or becomes painful, please bring him back in as those may be signs of infection," Dr. McQuarrie said.

"Right," Ashin said.

"Any other questions for me?" Dr. McQuarrie asked.

"At the end of the week, we bring him back in, and you'll take the stitches out?" June asked.

"Me, or almost anyone here. If they look good, a medical assistant can remove them, it's very quick. Or even your regular healthcare provider can do it. You needn't return to emergency services for that," Dr. McQuarrie said.

June nodded, and stood. "Thank you, doctor," June said.

"You bet. Bye Mateo," Dr. McQuarrie said, smiled, and left.

June hugged Mateo, picked up her bag, and turned to leave. Ashin followed June and Mateo to the door, and out into the lot. They climbed into the car, with Ashin behind the wheel.

"Want some ice cream or something?" June asked.

"Naw, I want to go see if my blood is still on the beach," Mateo said.

Ashin shook his head.

June said, "Mateo, my word."

"Maybe crabs have found it! Like, I'm being eaten by crabs right now!" Mateo said.

June put her face in her hands, and Ashin said, "Mateo, cool it a bit, huh?"

Mateo shrugged, and they headed home.

* * *

The next morning, Ashin decided he would indeed drop in on Deepak Funk, or at least try to. As much as he wanted to let a father know that his son had been hurt, and that he was alright, he was also curious about what was happening to the man.

He drove across town, and passed where he had first set up his practice. Normal strip-mall stuff: a consignment shop, a candle store, a dollar store where nothing cost less than $3, and a bookstore, that had bet everything on selling Christian-fundamentalist titles in a town where cookbooks would have sold much better.

He pulled into the parking lot of the apartment building, and parked next to a 1978 Ford LTD, with a boot on the front, right tire. The air was different here, on the east side of the wooded hills. Ashin went up the stairs to the apartment, and knocked on the door.

There was no response. The possibility was, of course, a real one, that Deepak wouldn't be home. Ashin knocked again, and said, "Deepak, it's Ashin Asilomar."

"Are you alone?" came Deepak's voice from within.

"I am. I didn't bring Mateo with me," Ashin said, thinking the chances of Deepak opening the door would be diminished.

"No police?" Deepak asked

Ashin stepped away from the door, and said, "It's just me." He was no longer entirely sure he wanted to go inside, and was feeling pretty smart that he had let June know where he was going.

There was the sound of locks being undone, and other noises, before the door opened a few inches. Ashin waited to see Deepak's face appear in the space, but it did not.

"Close the door behind you once you're in," Deepak said from inside.

Ashin slowly entered, scanning for the man but could not see him, and closed the door behind him.

"Lock the deadbolt at least," Deepak said from around a corner.

Ashin did, and then Deepak appeared. He looked remarkably normal. He was not wearing a tinfoil hat, nor paper pants. Instead, just a navy-blue T-shirt, and grey sweatpants. He was barefoot.

"What can I do for you?" Deepak asked.

"Do for me?" Ashin asked, looking around. There were indeed sandbags, lining the exterior walls, perhaps three feet high. Still, there were no weapons visible, and no gasoline cans or anything of the like. Ashin thought that was a good sign.

"Why did you come?"

"Mateo was accidentally hurt yesterday, and needed a few stitches," Ashin said.

"Why didn't he call, or his mother?" Deepak said.

"Well, it seems you've been a bit unpredictable lately, and I told June I'd come let you know," Ashin said.

"Mateo didn't want to come?" Deepak asked.

"I doubt Mateo knows I'm here," Ashin said.

"Where was he injured?

"On the beach," Ashin said.

"I mean, on his body. Where are the stitches?"

"Oh, I'm sorry, on his cheek," Ashin said. He was hoping he would not have to reveal that a bullet grazed the boy's face.

"And he'll be alright?"

Ashin said, "Absolutely fine." Ashin looked around the room again.

Deepak said, "I know this looks strange."

Ashin said, "It looks like you're preparing for a flood, but being on the second floor, I'm guessing not. That and this part of California worries much more about drought."

"It's not about water," Deepak said.

"So, why the sandbags?"

Deepak looked around, as if trying to remember why he had placed those bags there, and then said, "It's not like I'm expecting a SWAT team to attack or anything. I know all this wouldn't stop that sort of thing anyway. The sandbags are just reassuring and comforting in a way."

Ashin asked, "How so?"

"Remember when you were a child? Sometimes kids have a special blanket. No kid believes a cheap, fleece blanket could stop an attack from the monster under the bed, but still he feels safer within the blanket, or even under it," he said.

Ashin put his hand on top of the sandbag knee-wall, and said, "That's a heavy blanket."

"It's not a forcefield or anything, you know a piece of cloth can't stop the monsters, and pulled over your head, you can't even see them coming. And yet, it's somehow soothing," Deepak said.

"Are you planning to stay in this blanket for a long time?" Ashin asked.

"Actually, I've been leaving it for longer and longer trips to the 'outside' lately. I was out for almost twelve minutes yesterday," he said.

"Shouldn't you talk to someone, Deepak? Like a professional?" Ashin said.

"I'm already doing that work without one of those. They just ask you questions from a checklist and help you heal yourself. I'm asking myself the same questions," he said.

"They must do more than that," Ashin said.

"The ones who deviate most from that 'guiding-questions' script are likely deluded into some psycho-fad—flashing lights, beepers, the latest meds. Really, I'm guiding myself, and I've been capturing my thoughts," Deepak said.

"Capturing your thoughts?" Ashin asked.

"I wrote them down, writing them down, almost done," Deepak said.

"Deepak..." Ashin began.

"It's not like it's a manifesto, or whatever. It's just a declaration of my views and observations," Deepak said.

"I think that is literally what a manifesto is," Ashin said.

"Look, well, maybe, but I'm not holed up in a remote cabin in Montana," Deepak said.

Ashin looked around at the sandbag perimeter within the apartment.

"And I should probably get back to it," Deepak said.

"Is there anything I can do for you? Is there something you need?" Ashin said.

"I can walk to the market next door. You could tell Mateo to call me," Deepak said.

"I'll let him know," Ashin said.

"And don't come back here," Deepak said.

"What?" Ashin said.

"I don't want you to come back here. I see you—judging, measuring distances from wall to wall, trying to guess the temperature in the room. Well, I vary it! No one can ever predict exactly what temperature to expect in here," Deepak said.

"Okay, okay," Ashin said, "I won't say a word about any of this."

"Go on, go home," Deepak said.

Ashin nodded and walked to the door. Opening it, he turned and said, "I hope you'll get some help. For the boy, if for no other reason."

"Mateo doesn't need anything else from me. Go on, go," Deepak said.

Ashin hesitated, but then stepped out. The door closed behind him, and the sound of locks came again.

29

Almost a week later, Ashin was sitting in his living room, waiting for the Town Council meeting to begin on the television. There was a knock on the door, and then Mateo entered. Black stitches were visible on his cheek, with the bandage long gone.

"What are you doing?" Mateo asked.

"About to watch the council. They're going to discuss the housing issue. Pretty boring stuff. What are you doing here?" Ashin said.

"Mom has been talking to my father on the phone. He keeps hanging up, and then calling back," Mateo said.

Ashin worried he had agitated the disturbed man with his visit, and made it worse for June, and by extension, for Mateo.

"Have a seat. Watch some dull government stuff with me," Ashin said.

"Sounds good! Hey… can you take these out?" Mateo asked.

"The stitches?" Ashin asked.

"It's been six days. They itch, but they don't hurt. I can even move them," Mateo said.

Ashin looked closely. The wound was nicely healed; the doctor had done a fine job. The scar was a thin pencil line, and on such a young face would fade. Ashin asked, "Do you think your mother would mind?"

"If she does, I'll tell her I cut them out myself. You got some scissors?" Mateo asked.

"Looks like 6-O and pretty tight sewing. I don't think the kitchen Fiskars are the way to go. I'll be right back," Ashin said, and he went into the bathroom. Under the sink, he had his bag, and from that he pulled a pair of Spencer scissors, and small forceps. He rinsed them in alcohol, grabbed a couple gauze pads just in case, and returned to the living room where, on television, the meeting was just getting underway.

Ashin said, "Come here in the good light, and don't move."

Mateo asked, "Will this hurt?"

"Shouldn't. If it does, tell me," Ashin said. He snipped the first suture, and it easily slid free in the forceps.

"Ew," Mateo said.

"Hurt?" Ashin asked.

"Just feels weird," Mateo said.

On the television, the developer Cyrus Eliason, was called upon to present his latest proposal for housing. Eliason stood, walked over to a large covered flip chart, and began to speak.

"As I'm sure you remember, I came with an initial proposal, which you felt didn't serve families with children well enough," Eliason said.

"All one-bedroom apartments," one council member said.

"That's right. So, next, I returned with an updated proposal which added some larger family units," Eliason said.

"But not enough of them. We were looking for more of a community feel," another council member said.

"So you told me. I have new proposal," Eliason said, and removed the cover from the flip chart. The camera zoomed in on the image, and then focused. There was a large circular structure, like a wooden dome, with a hole in the top. It looked like the roof of a stadium with no seats inside—instead the roof went nearly to the ground.

"What is it?" asked a council member.

Ashin removed another stitch, and then another, but Mateo seemed to be transfixed by the image of the circular structure on the TV.

Eliason said, "You were very clear on wanting families to come to Paris, I thought you might prefer this sort of communal living. The Yanomami people in South America live in these, they're called *yanos* or *shabonos*. Some can hold as many as 400 people, with this open central area used for feasts and games."

"You're not serious," a council member said.

"Why not? No reason to worry about bedrooms and units. Each family gets their own hearth with which to cook, but there are no interior walls. They all raise the children together, as a community. At night, they climb into their hammocks to sleep," Eliason said.

"Are you mocking this council?" a council member asked.

"I am not," Eliason said.

"So, you'll be their chief then?" a council member asked, and then snorted.

"Oh no! The Yanomami believe fiercely in equality, and never have anything like a chief," Eliason said.

Just then, Boothby Baxter walked in wearing a T-shirt and jeans.

"We didn't think you'd be attending tonight, Mr. Baxter," said a council member.

"I didn't either," Boothby Baxter said, he made no movement toward his chair, and looked over at the flip chart.

"It's a yano," Eliason said.

"Lovely," said Boothby Baxter, and then he turned to the council and said, "I hereby resign, effective immediately."

"How will we tell the difference? We haven't seen you in some time," a council member said.

"Ah, well, it's official now," Boothby Baxter said, "No one can run this town anyway. Everyone has gone nuts. I'm receiving more than 300 emails per day, all of them complaints, each weirder than the last. I've had enough."

A council member asked, "Where will you go?"

Boothby Baxter smiled and said, "Fishing." He turned to Eliason and said, "Good luck with your yamo."

"It's a yano," Eliason said.

"Of course," Boothby Baxter said, and walked out.

There was silence. Ashin stopped removing Mateo's stitches.

"Wow," Mateo said.

"No kidding," Ashin said.

"Does he really want to build a yano?" Mateo asked.

"Who knows?"

A council member cleared his throat, and then asked, "Mr. Eliason, I'm not sure…"

Eliason interrupted and said, "Well, if you're not sure, I'll just take my yano and go. It's certainly been a pain in the ass dealing with you lunatics. I hope, at some point, you figure out exactly what it is you want." Eliason walked out, just as Boothby Baxter had, abandoning his flip chart.

"I move we adjourn," said one.

"Second," said another.

Ashin turned off the television, and removed Mateo's last stitch.

"Want to walk down to the carousel tomorrow?" Mateo asked.

"It's still closed," Ashin said.

"I know, but I want to go down that way," Mateo said.

Ashin said, "Sure, want me to drop by in the morning?"

"Not too early. Thanks for pulling those out of my face," Mateo said, rubbing it.

"You'll have to start taking showers again," Ashin said.

"It's better than baths. I've never been crazy about showers, but at least you feel clean after. With the tub, I feel like I step in dirty, turn my dirt into mud, lay in it until it gets cold, and when I stand up I'm still coated in it. Then I rub it with a dry towel, and put on pajamas. Seems like a waste of water and perfectly clean PJs," Mateo said.

Ashin smiled, and said, "I prefer showers, too."

Mateo stood up and headed for the door, and said, "See you in the morning, and thanks again." He gave his cheek a rub.

"See you then," Ashin said.

30

The next morning, Ashin walked across the lawns and onto the Funk's porch. He knocked, and heard June call for him to come inside, which he did.

"Hello," Ashin called into the house.

"Be right there," Mateo said.

June appeared, and said, "Good morning, and thank you for removing Mateo's stitches. I sometimes forget that you have experience with such things."

"You're welcome," Ashin said.

"Mateo tells me that the Town Council meeting got a bit strange last night?" June asked.

"I think the developer may have been having a bit of fun with them," Ashin said.

"Who were the people he mentioned again? From South America?" June asked.

"The Yanomami," Ashin said.

"Why bother coming to the meeting? Why not just call, and say he was pulling out?" June asked.

"I sense he was a bit frustrated," Ashin said.

"Speaking of frustration, did you hear about the new leather shop?" June asked. Mateo came out of his room.

"I didn't," Ashin said.

"After they gave that poor Shelley so much trouble about foreign leather, and animal rights, and whatever else, she decided to use a synthetic product, a faux leather, made right here in the United States," June said.

"And?"

"State health officials came and shut her down! Turns out the particular pleather she was using is toxic. It was making people sick. Not only a rash right where it contacted skin, but fever, headache, and nausea," June said.

"When do leather garments actually make contact with the skin?" Ashin asked. He had owned a leather jacket once, but he couldn't imagine leather on bare skin.

"Oh, pants, hats, shoes, gloves…" June said.

"Oh sure, gloves," Ashin said.

"And that freaky underwear," Mateo said.

"Mateo!" June said.

"You've got some," Mateo said.

His mother's face went red, and Ashin said, "Let's go." Mateo led Ashin out the front door.

"Why did you do that?" Ashin asked.

"What?" Mateo asked.

"Intentionally embarrass your mother," Ashin said.

Mateo didn't answer at first, and then he shrugged and said, "I don't know. It just came out."

"You should think before you talk. Remember what I said about having class," Ashin said.

"It just happens. I say things and do things, and then I wonder… why did I do that?" Mateo said.

"You should work on it," Ashin said.

"How does fake leather make people sick?" Mateo asked.

"Not all fake leather does. This stuff was probably soaked in something, and when people wear it, that chemical is absorbed by their bodies," Ashin said.

Mateo said, "They should've just let her sell what she wanted to in the first place."

"That's probably true. Especially since a bunch of those people ran for office promising to finally bring new businesses to Paris," Ashin said.

"Then why did they make it so hard for her?" Mateo asked.

"Because a lot of times we all agree on where we want to go, but can't agree on how to get there," Ashin said.

"What do you mean?" Mateo said.

"Most people agree on what problems need to be fixed, but they all have their pet projects and agendas, and it complicates everything. We spend a lot of time blocking each other's solutions to the problems we all agree we want to fix," Ashin said.

"But that lady with her dog problem," Mateo said.

"While everyone was fighting over real problems, and how to fix them, Almira and her little band invented a new problem, and suggested a fix to the problem, before anyone thought it through. The council basically went with what she said because they didn't really care either way, and it would make them look like they were accomplishing something. She just kept coming back, and when folks started to resist, she threatened lawsuits," Ashin said.

Mateo was shaking his head, and then said, "Look at all these fences. That park was so nice. And the beach was nice, too. But then, first you couldn't get to it, and then those guys tried to put a dam on it. Leather pants that make you sick, and a guy who wants to build a giant home that people from the jungle live in. No one can afford to buy a house anymore, and you can't even walk a dog."

"And you got shot in the face," Ashin said.

"Ricochet," Mateo said, "but this whole place needs to start over."

"A fresh start would be nice," Ashin said. "Part of why America is so much better than Europe was, when we created it, we knew all the problems in Europe, and we got a fresh start here."

"We stole the land, and made it work because we had slaves," Mateo said.

"Okay, but I was simply agreeing with you that a clean slate sometimes is the way to go," Ashin said. Looking around, he had to admit that Paris had transformed itself in a remarkably short time period. They arrived at the carousel.

"That's such a big building," Mateo said.

"Can you imagine, all the people building it, one board at a time?" Ashin said.

Mateo led the way, and they walked completely around the huge structure, all covered in white, wooden clapboards. "How long did it take to build?" Mateo asked.

"Actually, I don't know, but with teamwork, they used to be able to build pretty amazing things fairly quickly," Ashin said.

Mateo looked way up, and then said only, "Cool." And then he headed back toward home.

"Is that it?" Ashin asked.

"Where else could we go?" Mateo asked.

Ashin thought about it. Most of the best places were either difficult or impossible to get to. He said, "I guess you're right. We could work on the puzzle."

Mateo didn't answer. He just kept walking.

"What's on your mind?" Ashin asked, following the boy.

Mateo didn't answer at first, and then asked, "Have you ever built anything?"

"You mean like a house?" Ashin asked.

"Anything, like with wood or bricks or whatever," Mateo said.

Ashin thought for a moment. He'd built a practice, a career, a good reputation, a nice life with Rebecca, but he'd bought the house, and never really built anything in the sense Mateo was asking. "I suppose I haven't. Why?"

"It must be something, to create something that others can see and touch, that will last until after they're gone," Mateo said.

"Does art count?" Ashin asked.

"Why? Did you do something artistic?" Mateo asked.

"No, I was just wondering if it had to be a brick building, or if a painting would count," Ashin said.

Mateo kicked at a pebble, and then said, "I suppose,

if the painting was useful to people as long as a building was, and as useful to as many people as a building was."

"Utils," Ashin said.

"What's that?" Mateo said.

"Well, I'm not an economist, but there's this thing called a 'util.' In economics, it's a way of giving something a score for utility, for putting a number on how happy something makes you," Ashin said.

"For example," Mateo pressed.

"What's your favorite ice cream?" Ashin asked.

"Cookies and cream, with the Oreos in it," Mateo said.

"Yuck," Ashin said.

"You don't like Oreos? What's your favorite ice cream?" Mateo asked.

"Butter pecan is the best ice cream, by far," Ashin said, and smiled.

"That's old-people ice cream. Tell me about utils," Mateo said.

"Okay, so when you, Mateo, eat cookies and cream, that gives you, let's say, ten points worth of happiness. But when you eat butter pecan ice cream, you get only four points of happiness from it," Ashin said.

"Let's say two points," Mateo said.

"Okay, two. You get two utils from butter pecan, and ten utils from the Oreo ice cream," Ashin said. "Get it?"

"Why do they need to score happiness?" Mateo asked.

"For comparison's sake, just like what I did with the ice cream. Economics is the study of choices people make, and why."

"So, back to buildings and paintings?" Mateo said.

"So, let's say a reasonable person was given a building, and the same day, they were given a painting. Do you think it's possible to get the same amount of utils from receiving a painting as one would from receiving a building? Assuming there was no sentimental attachment to either?" Ashin said.

"By attachment you mean the building and the painting weren't attached to special memories, or someone they love, or something?" Mateo asked.

"Exactly," Ashin said.

Mateo thought for a moment, and said, "I guess most people would get more utils from being given a building, even if it cost the same amount of money as a famous painting."

"Seems reasonable to assume that. I mean, some people would say it's the art that gives them more joy, and come up with a bunch of flowery language to make themselves look fancy, but most people would be lying. They'd only be trying to stand out as more sophisticated," Ashin said.

"Or just to be different, like the kid who claims to love Brussels sprouts when every other kid is saying they hate them," Mateo said.

"Right!" Ashin said, "Wait, so, you don't like Brussels sprouts?

"I love them. Why?" Mateo said.

Ashin shook his head. "Never mind. But there is something different about art. You said you thought it would be possible for art to be considered as useful as a building, to represent as many utils, to just as many people, and for just as long."

"Possible, but hard to imagine a painting could do all that, though" Mateo said.

"I agree," Ashin said, "But maybe that's part of the point. There's something special about any kind of art. Think about it. If a fire breaks out at a famous museum, people rush in to save the art. They think of the art first."

"Well, if there are artistic masterpieces, those can't be replaced. A new building could be built," Mateo said.

Ashin said, "The Louvre opened as a museum in 1791. It was a palace before that, dating back hundreds of years. It's not exactly expendable. But you're right, people would still try to save the art. I mean, I can't imagine someone grabbing the Mona Lisa and trying to beat flames out with it, in order to save the building."

"Do you think a carpenter would look at a building he built, in the same way that a painter would look at his own painting?" Mateo asked.

"I do, I really do. But how would the general public look at each?" Ashin asked. "A moment ago, you said a building could be replaced. I think the average person looks at a thing differently than its creator does."

Mateo thought for a moment, and then said, "You know what's weird? Kids are pushed away from both?"

"What do you mean?" Ashin asked.

"Kids are pushed away from creative stuff, like painting and sculpting and music, and kids are also pushed away from being carpenters and other people who build things. Like with bricks and electricity and pipes. Parents push us towards like being lawyers or working with finance or whatever," Mateo said.

"Well, part of that is the amount of money you can

make, the wear and tear on your body, and the social circles you'll be in," Ashin said, and remembering Mateo's singing, "Did you get pushed away from music?"

Mateo ignored the part about his singing, and said, "But think about the public, and utils, like you said. How many utils does the public get from a person writing a legal paper for the court? Or how many utils will my children get from my mom's work in finance? Like, if I have a kid someday, will I show them a printout and say, 'Look, your grandmother built this algorithm.' Do you think it's the same as someone driving past a stone church who says, 'Look, your grandfather built that with his bare hands'?"

"I don't think the only utils that society derives from a lawyer is a paper in court. Some of our best and brightest people have worked with the law to right injustices, to save lives, to change minds and entire systems, and to set people free," Ashin said.

Mateo stopped walking, plopped down on the curb, and said, "That's probably true."

Ashin didn't sit, but he bent, placing his hands on his knees, and asked, "What's on your mind today?"

Mateo looked up and said, "I was only thinking, when you talked about the carousel building, and how people came together to build it... it must have been incredible to share it, but then someday when it comes down, it must be terribly sad."

"I suppose it is. All part of the cycle, though, I suppose. I imagine someone who puts up a building understands better than anyone how it could come down in its own good time, and that they hope that people make the most of it while it's there. That's why it's sad to me that it's not being used," Ashin said.

Mateo stood up and sad, "Yeah, that's true. The building, as it is, is kind of sad, isn't it?"

Ashin looked back the way they had come, and said, "It is."

Mateo brushed off his bottom, and started walking home again, and Ashin followed, again.

31

Ashin was sitting on his front porch at dusk when he saw the boy take off on his little bicycle, the rear basket clinking with Mason jars. After the first stroke or two of pedals, sheets of paper, stapled together fell from the basket. Mateo was halfway down the street before Ashin could call after him.

He stood, and thought about taking the car, but instead walked in the direction that Mateo had gone. Ashin stopped at the fallen papers, picked them up, and read the title page aloud, "Human Society and its Future." Ashin flipped through it. It was written by Deepak Funk.

It was tempting to begin reading, to see what Mateo had read, but Ashin rolled it, and stuck it in a back pocket. He thought it was more important to catch up with the boy. He anxiously walked in the direction Mateo had gone.

It wasn't long before Ashin heard the first siren, and his heart sank. He quickened his pace. Soon, there were a lot of sirens, and in the growing dark, Ashin could see a glow ahead. It was the carousel. Firetruck after firetruck was arriving, hooking up to every available hydrant, but the huge, old, wooden structure, which had long protected the carousel and all the candy shops, was soon fully involved.

Ashin scanned among the many onlookers for Mateo. The smoke hung heavy, the flames increasing in intensity. Firefighters were ordering people to back up, and were soon joined by the Paris Police Department in crowd control. People were asking questions like, “Did anyone see how it started?”

Waves of intense heat hit Ashin, and he stared into the fire, wondering if Mateo were somehow inside there. And then, he spotted him, coming out of the smoke. He jogged to the boy, who was wracked with coughing.

“Are you okay?” Ashin asked.

Old wood was popping, and embers were floating on the wind toward other structures. It was only a matter of time, and then someone yelled, “The old sandwich shop is on fire!” Firefighters were split now, as help arrived from surrounding towns. Ambulances arrived, too. Embers began falling all around them, like glowing, orange snow.

Mateo coughed, and croaked, “I’m okay.”

Afraid to ask, Ashin did anyway. “Did you see how it started?”

Mateo nodded, and said, “I used these.” He held up a Mason jar Molotov cocktail. Filled with gasoline, a rag stuffed in through a hole he had punched in the lid.

“Get rid of that!” Ashin snapped, looking around.

Mateo immediately flung it into a nearby rocky ditch, where it shattered. Embers fell into it and the gasoline ignited in a whoosh. Embers also ignited the garage just beyond the ditch. A hot ember fell on Ashin's arm, and he hissed. "Let's back up from here."

They moved a distance away, and then a police officer approached. Mateo was coughing when the officer got to them, and asked, "Is he okay?"

"He's got cystic fibrosis, and the smoke isn't helping," Ashin said.

The officer said, "Hey, it's you! All healed up, huh?"

Ashin recognized the police officer as the one that Mateo had insisted shot him.

Mateo said, "The scar isn't even that big."

"They did a nice job stitching you up,' the officer said. "You both should probably head home. This is spreading. I'm suddenly glad I couldn't afford to buy here."

Ashin asked, "Any idea how it started?"

The flames were roaring now, making their own wind, and Ashin could see at least two houses on fire.

"We'll probably never know. Probably just that old building's turn to go, and it's going to take some others with it," the officer said, "There are reports of some guy, running around here like a lunatic."

Ashin looked around, but mostly he just saw the crowd disbursing, and firefighters in a desperate and losing fight.

The officer said again, "Really, folks, you should head home. Pack a little overnight bag. No telling how bad this will get."

"Thanks, be safe," Ashin said. He physically turned

Mateo, and they began walking home.

Firefighters pulled up beside a home where the fire was just taking hold on its roof. They hooked up to the hydrant, but couldn't get close enough, because of the huge fences, to spray the part of the roof that was igniting. One firefighter began cutting through the chain-link fence, when another shouted, "Don't do it! Look at the signs! Landmines!"

The firefighter stopped trying to cut his way in. Just then, Ashin heard screaming and maniacal laughter. He and Mateo looked back, and silhouetted against the wall of flame was Deepak Funk, running around in circle, laughing, waving his arms over his head.

"Dad!" Mateo shouted.

Deepak stopped, waved one hand at Mateo, and then ran into the smoke, arms waving above his head.

Mateo dropped his shoulders, and then Ashin and Mateo kept walking.

In a low voice, Ashin asked, "Why? Why did you do this?"

"The town needed a fresh start. A clean slate," Mateo said.

"My God, Mateo, people might be killed," Ashin said.

"I hope not," Mateo said, matter-of-factly.

Ashin brought Mateo home, and entered, calling out for June. Mateo was still coughing, while Ashin explained everything. June sat hard in a chair.

Mateo said, "Sorry, Mom."

June stood up, and said, her voice absolutely flat, "Go pack, fill your two suitcases, and grab your games."

Mateo went without a word.

"Will you help us carry stuff to the car?" June asked.

"It'll look suspicious," Ashin said.

"It'll only look like we were escaping the fire. You probably should be ready to go, too," she said.

"Where will you go?" Ashin asked.

"I'm not entirely sure. My office goes with me, so I can go anywhere. I'll be in touch. Do you think your friend Mitch can help sell this house?" June asked.

"We have no idea what tomorrow's going to bring," Ashin said as two more firetrucks, sirens blaring, raced by toward the center of town.

June said, "Right, right."

Ashin added, "But I'll call him. He sold his home and is moving, but he probably can set you on the right path."

"Thank you," June said.

Her voice was so calm, it only worried Ashin more. "You okay to drive?"

"I'll process all this later, probably cry hysterically for a couple days, but for right now I have to get Mateo out of here," June said, and she headed for the hallway.

Ashin just stood there for a moment, and then stepped outside. The glow from the fire made it clear that there might be a dozen buildings burning. "A fresh start," Ashin said, shaking his head. How could someone not be hurt in all that?

June and Mateo began bringing stuff out, and June said to Ashin, "The rest of the stuff is inside, and right by the door."

Ashin went in, and found five more bags of various sizes. Picking up the largest three, he immediately put one of them back down, and carried the two bags out to the car.

"Please, put those in the backseat," June said, and she headed back inside. A police car slowly drove up the road, lights flashing, and through a bullhorn, the officer inside said, "Everyone must evacuate. Everyone must go. Take just a few bags and your pets, and get out of Paris. Do not try to stay and fight the fire. You will only be in the way. Everyone must evacuate."

June and Mateo returned with the last of the bags, and also put those in the back seat. Then June turned to Ashin, "Thank you for everything. We'll be in touch."

"I'm not sure you will be, but I hope so," Ashin said, and went to one knee.

"I'll definitely be in touch," Mateo said. "I want to go back to that talk we had about utils, and maybe how many utils nothing is worth."

"Nothing is worth?" he asked, accepting Mateo's hug. Ashin felt his nose burning, as if he might cry. He let Mateo go, and saw that there were tears on the boy's cheeks, but his face was almost… peaceful.

Ashin wiped a tear on Mateo's face.

Mateo said, "It's just the smoke. I'll call you. I'll probably even come back."

June said, "Let's get in the car, Mateo."

"If I can find a way," Mateo said.

"Take care," Ashin said.

"You too," Mateo said, and climbed into the car.

"Be careful," Ashin said to them both, and without another word, June drove away.

The fire was closer. Ashin walked to his own driveway,

made sure his car was locked in the garage, went inside, and turned off every light and closed every curtain but one. He pulled a chair up to the window, and watched as the police came by again, ordering everyone to evacuate.

* * *

Throughout the night, as Ashin watched the fire grow closer, he saw a few resident refugees leaving, and he watched the firefighters battle valiantly, in retreat. Only when the house directly across the street caught fire did Ashin feel a pang of concern, but then it faded. *Whatever happens, happens*, he thought. Then he could see just enough to know that the Glerter house was on fire.

The closed windows weren't holding out all of the smoke, and Ashin wondered how tough things would get. He walked over and picked up Rebecca's jewelry box, turned the little silver key on the bottom, and sat near a window. He opened the lid, and "Greensleeves" began to play. He considered lighting the jasmine candle, but then remembered it was long gone, and there was perhaps enough fire anyway.

Just then, three firetrucks came onto his and the Funk's lawn, and hooked into the hydrant. With no fences nor minefields to contend with, they appeared to have decided that this was the place to make a stand. Sheets of water fell on the road between the firefighters and the fire, and looking out his own windows was like looking through a waterfall. A lone firefighter came up the stairs and pounded on Ashin's door, twice, and then rejoined the others. The three firetrucks and their personnel had, in essence, created a dome around themselves, his house, and the Funk house.

Ashin thought that as long as the water held out, his house might make it through. The music from the jewelry box continued to play, but it was slowing. Gently closing the lid, Ashin watched the firefighters a bit longer, but then retrieved a small flashlight, pulled Deepak's manifesto from his pocket, opened it to a random page, and began to read.

> As I was saying on the previous page, even the idea of perfect is subjective. We would expect all perfection to be objective, but listen to how people explain the discovery of the perfect situation or thing or place. "I think it's perfect," they say, or even, "It's perfect for us."
>
> Of course, all words cheapen over time. People claim to "love" something or someone when they are simply expressing a moment of appreciation or gratitude.
>
> Example:
>
> P1- "How about extra cheese on the pizza?"
>
> P2- "I love it!"
>
> If Person2 then tells his wife that he "loves" her, he's used the same exact word as he did for cheese. So, perhaps the word "perfect" has been cheapened, and is no longer a superlative. Perfection has

become relative. Some place might be "even more perfect" than the last place.

If true, we run into the same problem with every other evaluation. How do we express to others what it is we are experiencing? There can't be empirical validation of perfection if the next thing might be more perfect.

My son spoke to me about people moving to a town they claimed was perfect, and then they felt they needed to make some improvements. He wondered why they had called it perfect in the first place.

Maybe the newcomers thought the new town had the potential to be perfect, but hadn't attained that yet. It calls to mind that the newcomers must feel that they, and not the townspeople, are uniquely suited to observe that the town is not yet perfect, and why it isn't, and that it should be changed. The very environment that the town's residents had created attracted the newcomers, but the newcomers thought the townspeople had yet to maximize the potential of the town, and that the locals needed the newcomers to catalyze the changes.

However, the changes actually lower the level of perfection in the eyes of those who were already there. The

> locals complain that the newcomers are "messing it all up." Still, the locals are less likely to make waves, or to resist. They are not the change agents; the newcomers are. While the locals ask, "Can't we all just get along?" the newcomers are actively petitioning local officials, organizing, and even running for office. Thwarted, they file lawsuits.

Ashin stopped reading for a moment, and said, "It's not just the new people," and thought of Almira.

> Most of the locals are pre-reflectively conscious of the changes, but won't really understand what is being lost until it's too late. There will be a few locals who will, in real time, try to warn everyone, but they'll be regarded as kooks in the wilderness. After the town's character is lost, it's history, a memory, its guiding principles co-opted, it'll be too late to "go back to how things were."
>
> Many of the locals will actually leave, and look for another place that was like the place they lost to the newcomers, saying that the town they've loved "just isn't the same anymore." If the newcomers succeed in changing the town too much, turning it into the town they left in search of perfection, they too

> will then leave. In the aftermath, those who remain will wistfully recall how the town was back when it was perfect.
>
> Even they will run into the limits of intersubjectivity. They, as a collective group, are remembering different realities, different perfections.

Ashin thought, *where's he going with this?* He looked out into the dark, the artificial dome of rain, and it seemed the fire might be dying simply for lack of fuel. He returned to the document.

> So, how do we deal with all this subjectivity, and delay of recognition, reflection, and consciousness? We have to peel situation back to a point where there can be no subjectivity. We need to reduce to a point where there is nothing to interpret.

Ashin heard a distant crash, looked out, but couldn't see anything.

> All we can agree on is absence. With anything present, we will try to judge, understand, and measure. However, if there is nothing but absence, we can finally establish an intersubjective without any chance of misinterpretation or miscommunication. The only possible

> thought, deduction, inference, is that there is absence.
>
> Therefore, the obvious answer to any strife is simply to wipe everything away, and start over. Worrying about the previous investment of resources, time, and effort is stuck thinking, and it doesn't allow the absence to occur. The memories of what existed in the past defeat the absence. Wipe it all away, burn it all down, and forget about it, and only then is there a intersubjectivity and a common understanding of what's left. Nothing.
>
> And nothing is better than nothing.

Good Lord, Ashin thought, *Mateo read this and put it into action. Deepak hadn't simply been raving at the fire, he was celebrating it.*

He started to read some more, but then closed it, and dropped it to the floor. Ashin thought of Mateo, and June, and what they will have to live with, especially if people are hurt.

The water that had been hitting his roof and windows suddenly stopped. He looked outside, and could see weary firefighters milling about. There were faint glows beyond the trees, but these firefighters were not rushing off, and instead they circled up next to one of the trucks. Ashin sat back in his chair. What was Paris going to look like at daybreak, he wondered? If someone had been killed, how would he feel about his young friend,

Mateo? Was he a murderer? A victim of life, and of his father's pen? Assuming no one was hurt, would Paris be better off, with its fences gone, and with much larger challenges than Almira's dog problems?

Ashin laid his head back, looked at the ceiling, and closed his eyes.

32

Ashin woke in the same chair by the window. There was complete silence. The house still stood around him. He rose, and began opening curtains. The Funk house looked fine, too. The firetrucks were gone, but both front lawns were completely trashed. They looked more plowed than mowed. Smoke hung everywhere in the air, creating a thick haze, but nothing seemed to be burning. As far as he could see, with the exception of the Funk's and his, every house had burned. Trees were blackened, and the road was coated in wet, black debris, mixed with mud.

He put on his shoes, grabbed a mask in case he found it hard to breathe, and went for a walk. House after house had burned to the ground. Many piles of rubble were not as high as the scorched fences that encircled them. As it turned out, although the smell of smoke was everywhere, it was not difficult to breathe. With the houses out of the way, Ashin could see the ocean much more easily than he had been able to in decades. He looked over to the Glerter's place, and it was nothing but debris. He headed for where the carousel had been, passing twisted fencing, and plastic charred globs that used to be stuffy-dog guardians. There were a few burned-out cars, their paint scorched, tires melted, and their windows broken, but not that many. None seem to have exploded, but instead were simply reduced and charred.

The carousel building was gone, and the carousel with it. A scorched and severed wooden horse's head lay in a permanent and silent scream, eyes wild. There was a man, in gloves, who was looking at the rubble, and taking notes. The man bent down suddenly, and lifted a charred and partially melted bicycle. Ashin knew it was Mateo's.

"What do you have there?" Ashin asked the man.

"I'm from the fire inspector's office, and it looks like a kid's bike," he said.

"A little kid's bike, like seven years old," Ashin said.

"Yup, looks like it," the inspector said, and made a note.

Ashin, looking around, asked, "Was anyone killed?"

"Can you believe it? Not a soul. There are half-a-dozen firefighters in the hospital, but all expected to recover," the inspector said.

"It's a miracle," Ashin said.

"You got that right," the inspector said.

Ashin spotted a large, brown, shiny puddle. "What is that?" he asked.

The inspector looked over and said, "Basically, it's caramel," and then he went back to work.

Ashin stared for a moment and then left, heading for the park. When he got there, he saw a large gap had been pulled open in the fences, and people with windbreakers were setting up large emergency tents. Trucks were arriving with cases of water and food. Grills were being set up. While there were perhaps fifty emergency aid personnel, there were only twenty-five or thirty residents of Paris in the park.

Most of the long-time residents had sold and moved away, and most of those who had bought had never moved in. Or, they were like the Glerters, who had lived in Paris just long enough to help ruin what they had called its perfection, and then had abandoned it.

Ashin looked around, and said, “It’s certainly not perfect now, Mateo, but maybe it is nothing.”

33

The next day, Ashin sat in his driveway in a lawn chair. The door to his car was open, and the radio was playing.

The song ended, and a news announcer said, "To update the Paris fire story, there are still no confirmed deaths as a result of the blaze. One woman, identified this morning as Dorothy Rieger, age seventy-three, was found on her porch, deceased, as officials went door to door in an effort to evacuate residents. Officials say that she did not die as a result of the smoke or fire, and no foul play is suspected."

Ashin sat straight at the news, remembered Dottie at the park, and how she had said he'd likely not see her again. Had she known she wasn't well? He was sad she hadn't lived to hear musicians in the park again, if they ever return. *Sometimes we hope for something, imagining all the variables lining up so it can happen, but we don't factor in whether or not we will be around to experience it when they do*, Ashin thought.

Ashin also thought of Deepak Funk. It seemed he

had apparently survived. Hopefully he was long gone; it seemed almost certainly officials would be looking for the crazy outsider, who was even seen at the scene where the fire started. If they question him, he'll likely go on about the power of the absence of everything, and his goose will be cooked.

"Authorities, of course, have not gone through every house, but they say they have been in touch with every homeowner, and no one appears to be missing. Seven firefighters were hospitalized, and six have already been released. The seventh is in stable condition, and is expected to recover. The cause of the fire is still under investigation. According to some estimates, sixty percent of the town of Paris has been lost, including the historic carousel," the announcer said.

Ashin hoped the investigation won't go on for too long. It certainly helped that no one was apparently killed.

"Hazmat teams are cleaning up one site in particular, however. It seems a faux-leather shop burned with a large quantity of toxic inventory on the premises. The public is asked to stay away from the leather shop on Milton Avenue," the announcer said. "Those who live near the shop, experiencing symptoms such as vomiting, or signs of blood when they cough, should seek medical attention immediately."

"Officials also ask that those who are not residents of Paris to please stay away. It seems that there are reports of individuals coming in, collecting mementos of the tragedy and selling those pieces online," the announcer said. "Investigators are trying to determine, case by case, who is selling those items, and referring those responsible to the Monterey County District Attorney's Office for decisions regarding possible prosecution."

"They just can't get enough of Paris. Now they're selling its ashes," Ashin said, shaking his head.

"It is likely that power and other utilities will take weeks to be restored, according to the California Office of Emergency Services. Representatives of all the major insurance companies are in Paris. The governor has declared Paris a disaster, and has requested federal aid as well. The slopes along Alta Mesa Road are unstable, and with the predicted rains, there is a risk of mudslides. The public is advised to avoid the area," the announcer said.

Ashin looked over his shoulder at his house, and then out at the lots he could see. He wondered how old his house, and the Funk's house, would look after insurance money came in and people rebuilt. Or would they, he wondered? He had heard of victims of fires waiting years for the insurance companies to pay the claims, and then another year waiting for contractors to become available. He wondered if he'd be the only resident in this part of town for the next few years.

He thought about it, and decided that it would no longer be enough to simply have the power come back on, and the sidewalks cleared enough for him to go for his walks. He had grown used to, and even quite fond of, Mateo's company, and while it wasn't painful like Rebecca's passing, Ashin knew he missed the boy.

He wasn't quite sure what to make of missing him, since Mateo was guilty of dozens of counts of felony arson, might well have killed scores of people if he and they hadn't gotten so remarkably lucky, and clearly the kid needed some serious psychiatric help. Even by not reporting what he knew, Ashin wondered if he, himself, was breaking the law.

Still, he did hope to see Mateo again. Maybe even to discuss Paris a few years after the fire, once they knew if the town was going to remain a charred slope to the ocean, or if it would be overrun by hotel and restaurant chains, or if it would once again become a place of family neighborhoods, with kids headed for the beach, and crossing lawns on their way. Of course, Ashin, especially with Dottie in mind, knew he had no idea how much time he had left. No one did.

In the meantime, Ashin thought he'd try to find a friend to walk with. Ashin opened the cooler beside him, took out a bottle of lemonade, and listened as the radio went back to music. He took a long drink and, as he lowered the bottle, he saw an unfamiliar young dog—no leash, of course—walking down the street.

AFTERWORD

For the record, I disagree with the idea that destruction down to absence is the only path to improvement. In fact, I think that's the easy way out. We need to fix the airplane in flight, and not resort to parachutes.

This doesn't mean we need to compromise with fascists, racists, and other haters, but Almira as portrayed in this story is not a Nazi. She's a bored, insecure bully with pull and resources looking for a purpose. The two idiots on the beach are scared and insecure, but are not fascists. The people erecting fences were acting reflexively to what they were seeing, out of fear and insecurity, because no one was benevolently leading.

We all want a purpose, we all want to feel heard and safe, we all want to feel significant. We can do that for each other. Fences and angry signs aren't the answer.

NOTICE

If you enjoyed this novel, we believe you might also like *Aliens, Drywall, and a Unicycle* by Kevin St. Jarre. Published by Encircle Publications, it is available in hardcover, paperback, and e-book, wherever good books are sold and from your favorite online bookseller.

At the end of this edition of *Paris, California*, the first chapter of *Aliens, Drywall, and a Unicycle*, has been included with our best wishes.

Acknowledgments

As always, thank you to the entire Encircle Publications team, and to artist Deirdre Wait for the cover. I love it.

Amy Libby, who gave Ashin his name, and whose optimism is contagious and seemingly unending.

Catherine Perreault, who let me know (while I was writing this book) that a popular TV series already had a character named Tobias Funke. Because of that, I changed the name of the character in this novel to Mateo. I had no idea of this when I originally named him Tobias Funk, and apparently the TV character is nothing like my character. A weird and frustrating coincidence, but I came to love the name Mateo.

While my first apartment was Apt #1 at 2905 David Avenue in Pacific Grove, California…the town of Paris in this book is NOT Pacific Grove. Instead, Paris is everywhere.

Thanks to ConvenientMD on Marginal Way in Portland, Maine, who quickly got me some Paxlovid when, halfway through writing this novel, I contracted COVID-19.

Excerpt from *Aliens, Drywall, and a Unicycle*

by Kevin St. Jarre

1

Unpacking is infinitely better than packing. When a person tries to fit his old life into boxes, it's an ongoing series of decisions about what gets abandoned and what does not.

Tom Tibbetts was unpacking. Bits of his old life appeared from the containers, settled into the corners of his new life, and filled the cramped apartment. The place smelled of fresh but cheap paint, new but bargain carpet, and Pine-Sol. The walls and the ceiling were white, and the same beige carpet ran through every room in the place. Tom had the interior door open, and a breeze coming in through the screen door did its best to push the smell of chemicals out the windows.

His life had imploded, leaving him hurt and cynical. The entire thing was quite complicated, he believed, and no one seemed to really understand. Eventually, he began to see everyone as either hostile, stupid, or some combination. He knew he wasn't likeable; he knew people couldn't sympathize. Remembering his father's saying, "If you meet more than two assholes in the same day, it's actually you who is the asshole," he understood where he stood. He just couldn't see the way back up.

He had taken a job in a college town, after the students had returned for the fall semester, and they had snapped up the better housing. Finding an apartment in the Cooper building, Tom was surrounded by neighbors. He was in apartment 2B in a three-story complex with nine units. His was the least desirable in the building, with neighbors above and below him, and on either side. Across the face of the building, at each floor, was a shared concrete balcony with a wrought-iron railing and stairs, and his door opened onto this. There was no interior stairwell.

Down on the street, someone Tom couldn't see, shouted, "Hey! Fuck you, douchebag!"

It was quite a change from his previous address, where he'd had a house with a yard, a stockade fence, and a trail down to the brook. The house had come with Vicky, and it had stayed with her. What he missed most was his old dog, Wallace. More than a few times, especially after one of the many nasty fights with Vicky, Tom had thought the dog was the only friend he had in the world.

Wallace had loved to chase a ball, and they'd spent many hours in the dog park, just the two of them. Over the years Wallace had slowed, turned grey, and Tom knew the inevitable was coming. The day Wallace died, he and Vicky had held each other crying, but when the next fight with Vicky came, Tom realized how alone he really was. It wasn't long after that day that Vicky gave him enough reason to leave.

In Portage, he had his new apartment, with no dog, and no girlfriend. He'd brought along two houseplants, but they didn't add any sort of comfort. Instead, at best they seemed like fellow refugees, and at worst, hostages.

However, he was not alone for long, and met his first neighbor before he was completely unpacked. She appeared at his doorway wearing cutoff jeans and a long-sleeve black shirt bearing the oft-seen photo of Kurt Cobain in the cardigan he wore for the MTV Unplugged gig. Pushing Kurt out of shape were two obviously unrestrained breasts. Her dark hair was long and curly, and her feet were bare. She wore heavy eyeliner but no other make-up.

"Hey," she said through the screen.

"Hey."

"You need anything, I'm on top of you," she said.

Tom said nothing, but then she pointed upward and said, "I'm in the apartment above you."

"Cute," Tom said, wondering how many times she'd rehearsed that, or used it on previous tenants. She grinned, and he smiled in spite of himself.

"What's your name?" she asked.

"What's yours?" Tom asked.

"Brynn," she said.

"Brynn what?"

"Just Brynn," she said.

"No last name?"

She grinned again, and then asked, "So, she threw you out?"

"Who?" Tom asked, but he knew who. Vicky hadn't so much as thrown him out as she had replaced him. Throughout her life, Tom knew, Vicky was always on the lookout for the next upgrade, but she was never single between men. Her relationships tended to overlap. Of course, a guy doesn't believe he'll be another one of those stories, or layers, until after it happens to him.

"Whoever got you that sweater," she said.

It was a lime green v-neck and Tom wasn't sure why it'd made the cut, even though it was his mother who'd given it to him years before.

"You want it?" he asked.

She giggled and leaned forward until first her breasts and then her forehead rested against the screen.

"You coming in?" he asked. "Or are you going to keep talking to me through the door?"

"I don't know you well enough yet," she said.

Looking her over, he knew there was no chance that she was as uncomplicated as she was trying to seem. Tom asked, "How old are you, Brynn?"

"Rude," she said, but then, "I'm twenty-three. How old are you?"

"I'm almost twenty years older than you," he said.

"I wasn't looking to hook up or anything," she said.

He said, "I wasn't implying that."

"You were checking me out a minute ago," she said.

"Was I?" he asked.

She said, "It's okay, men do that, but I wasn't looking to hook up. I've got a boyfriend."

He asked, "Is he a Nirvana fan too?"

"A what?" she asked.

"The shirt," he said.

She looked down at her chest. "Oh right, I'm not really a fan of the music."

"Why the shirt?" he asked, unable to help himself.

"I thought he went out really cool," she said.

Tom stopped unpacking, and said, "He was desperately depressed, chronically sick and in constant pain, addicted to heroin, and he blew his head off."

"If you believe he killed himself, which I do—I'm not one of those 'Courtney-killed-him-whackos' but he had the courage to go through with it and now he'll live always, and forever young and beautiful," she said.

"Abandoning his daughter," he said.

"Abandoning his millionaire daughter."

"I bet she'd trade those millions for more time with her dad," he said.

She paused, tilted her head, and then said, "Whatever. You a teacher or something?"

"What makes you think I'm a teacher?" he asked.

"Well, you don't look like you lift heavy shit for a living," she said.

"A reporter. I'm taking a job at the newspaper," he said. "And I'm a writer."

"Isn't a newspaper reporter a writer?"

"I also write books," he said.

"Heh. For Kindle and stuff?" she asked.

"For Kindle and stuff," he said.

"Cool. I read a lot," she said.

"You do?"

"Don't seem so surprised. Eyeliner and tits don't make you stupid, you know," she said.

She was beginning to ruin his good mood. He said, "Listen, I didn't mean anything by it. I'm just moving in, unpacking . . . busy."

"I get it," she said. "I'll let you get to it. But you did think about hooking up with me." She grinned again, and was gone from his doorway.

Tom blinked, stood there quietly for a moment, and wondered if all his neighbors were like Brynn.

Opening the next box, he pulled out four glasses, all different sizes. A small one he'd probably never use, a medium-sized plastic tumbler he would use to hold pens and pencils, a heavy pint glass, and a wine glass. Holding this last one, he looked around at the mess, abandoned the current box for another, and pulled out a bottle of Barolo and a corkscrew. He took the freshly poured glass out onto the balcony, leaned on the railing, and took a sip. The wine was warm and tannic, and the breeze smelled of asphalt. With the railing rocking on loose screws, Tom surveyed the view.

Portage, New Hampshire had been a mill town, but when the mill went silent, the town reinvented itself as a college town. The local school, once Portage State College, had grown to the point of joining the university system and had been reborn as Portage State University. It was hardly the same place. Once a town with sidewalks full of men carrying lunchboxes, and then a Main Street of shuttered shops through the tough years, Portage had become a town of young people, university events, yoga, coffee shops, and wandering grad students who never seemed to leave. From Tom's vantage point, he could see red brick, white vinyl siding, glass, pedestrians, small patches of green, and cars driving the short circuitous route that was the downtown. The entire vista sloped down to the river.

He looked forward to becoming a part of the community. Tom had been a reporter at a smaller newspaper, writing stories and occasionally contributing columns, until accepting the new position here at *The Portage Herald*.

"Are you a teacher or something?"

Tom turned and saw a man in his thirties, khaki shorts, and a loose button-down short-sleeve shirt, Birkenstocks, with a shaggy head of hair.

"Why a teacher?" Tom asked. Did he look that much like a teacher?

"It's the middle of a summer workday, and you're already drinking wine," he said, and smiled.

"Not a teacher," Tom said.

"I'm Ben, 2C," he said, thumbing back at his door.

"I'm Tom," he said and took another sip.

"Moving in?" Ben asked.

"Just about done. Just have to unpack the boxes," Tom said.

"What brought you here?" Ben asked.

Tom knew he'd be an object of curiosity for his new neighbors, but he thought it would look more like furtive glances and silent wondering. These people just walked up and started asking questions, as if in a rush to piece together some satisfying one-paragraph biography on the new guy. He knew, that whatever he said or did in reply supplied a puzzle piece. If he answered honestly and sincerely, that would provide info. If he answered curtly or snidely, that would provide info. If he silently went back into his apartment, that would provide info. Tom was a journalist, and he liked providing information, but about other people. Still, he was in a decent mood. Why not be friendly?

Tom smiled, and said, "I'm taking a job at the *Portage Herald*. I've been with the *Insider*. Did you go to school here?"

"I didn't go to school at all; I work at McDonald's," Ben said, and then added, a bit too loudly, "Want fries with that?"

Just as Tom was about to wonder if any of the neighbors would be able to participate in an intelligent conversation, Ben said, "Nope. No college I. I'm proud to say that I'm an autodidact."

Tom's eyebrows lifted; that was potentially interesting. "What have you taught yourself?" he asked.

Ben said, "Name it, man, I never stop learning. I can't get enough."

"You read a lot?"

Ben said, "Man, I read all the time. Whatever I can find. I also learn from the Internet, TV, and movies. I learn from people, too, man, 'cause even though I'm like fuckin' Chatty Cathy right now, I'm actually like an intense listener, you know? Like, I listen, man, I listen hard, and it sticks. I just get bored if I can't be in charge of what I'm learning, you know? Like, be in control of what's going into my head, you know?"

Tom's hopes were initially raised, but he was becoming a bit more skeptical.

"Tell me one thing you've learned. Impress me," Tom said.

"I don't learn shit to impress people, man. It's impossible to impress people, man. Even when people are impressed, it's so fucking uncool to be impressed with anything that no one will admit it, you know?" Ben said.

Tom smiled, nodded, and took another sip. So the guy heard the word "autodidactic" on Jeopardy or something and he's throwing it around now as an excuse for not furthering his education.

Ben said, "Alright, man, okay. How about this? I can speak Spanish."

"So can the better-prepared half of Americans," Tom said.

"Okay, man, but last Christmas, I could barely order in Taco Bell. Now, I speak Spanish, man."

"You speak Spanish," Tom said.

"I speak fluent Spanish, man. I watch movies in Spanish now and understand pretty much all of it. I know Russian too. I'm learning Latin now," Ben said.

Tom lowered his glass. "You know Russian."

"I'm not bullshitting you, man."

"Why are you learning languages?" Tom asked.

"Because otherwise when I read translations, there is an intermediary between me and the author, man, and they can't help but change it. Not just because of linguistic issues either, it's all about ego, man," Ben said. "All these far out ideas, but we get them filtered through some loser's biases before we get to experience them."

It did occur to Tom that this fast-food genius had just referred to others as losers. "Why do you work at McDonald's?"

"Why not work at McDonald's?" Ben asked. "Because people look down on it? I'm not going to switch jobs because of what other people think. I'm good at my job, and the people are friendly."

"But the pay," Tom said.

"Man, why are you looking for problems in my life? I make the money I need, and I spend the rest of my time learning and experiencing shit. Yeah, man, I'm not a kid anymore and I work at McDonald's, but I don't live in my mother's basement and I don't make a living building weapons or lying to people," Ben said.

Tom hadn't felt he was being negative, and said, "Look, I didn't mean…"

"You did mean it, man, but it's no thing. It's normal. We've been conditioned to be in a perpetually dissatisfied state, man, and we help each other maintain it," Ben said.

"The basis of ambition," Tom said.

"You say 'ambition' like it's a good thing, man," Ben said and grinned, and they both laughed.

"Look, man, you know the special sauce in Big Macs?" Ben asked.

"Thousand Island dressing. What about it?"

"Dude, see, exactly. Why? Why are you trying to take the 'special' out of the sauce? That's a myth, man. It's not Thousand Island dressing. Chefs working for McDonald's came up with that recipe. In fact, it changed over the years, but not that long ago, the CEO ordered everyone to go back to the original recipe and they had to find it, because it got deleted, so they did some intense detective work and tracked it down. If it were just Thousand Island, they could've just bought some at the supermarket."

"Okay, sorry," Tom said. "So, what about the special sauce?"

Ben took a breath, and seemed to relax again, "It's special because it was made for one thing, to be the special sauce on a special sandwich. McDonald's sells 550 million Big Macs every year in the United States alone, dude. Can you think of a more successful sauce than that?"

Tom said, "Ketchup."

Ben paused, and then burst out laughing. "Right on, man, right on."

"I should get back to unpacking," Tom said.

"Cool, cool," Ben said.

Nice meeting you," Tom said.

"You, too, Tom. I'll see you on the balcony," he said.

Tom went back into his apartment, drank the last of the glass of wine, and surveyed the work left to do.

About the Author

KEVIN ST. JARRE is also the author of *The Book of Emmaus* (2022), *Absence of Grace* (2022), *The Twin* (2021), *Celestine* (2021), and *Aliens, Drywall, and a Unicycle* (2020), all published by Encircle Publications. He previously penned three original thriller novels for Berkley Books, the Night Stalkers series, under a pseudonym. He's a published poet, his pedagogical essays have run in *English Journal* and thrice in *Phi Delta Kappan*, and his short fiction has appeared in journals such as *Story*.

Kevin has worked as a teacher and professor, a newspaper reporter, an international corporate consultant, and he led a combat intelligence team in the first Gulf War. Kevin is a polyglot, and he earned an MFA in Creative Writing with a concentration in Popular Fiction from University of Southern Maine's Stonecoast program. Twice awarded scholarships, he studied at the Norman Mailer Writers Center on Cape Cod, Massachusetts, with Sigrid Nunez and David Black, and wrote in southern France at La Muse Artists & Writers Retreat.

He is a member of Maine Writers & Publishers

Alliance, and International Thriller Writers. Born in Pittsfield, Massachusetts, Kevin grew up in Maine's northernmost town, Madawaska. He now lives on the Maine coast, and is always working on the next novel. For the latest news, follow Kevin at www.facebook.com/kstjarre, on Twitter @kstjarre, and visit www.kevinstjarre.net.

QR Code brings you to KevinStJarre.net:

www.ingramcontent.com/pod-product-compliance
Lightning Source LLC
Chambersburg PA
CBHW020329030826
48979CB00021B/507

* 9 7 8 1 6 4 5 9 9 4 0 7 7 *